13 WAYS TO RUIN YOUR LIFE

A PRACTICAL GUIDE FOR GUYS

JARROD JONES

GRESHAM HILL PUBLISHING
NASHVILLE, TENNESSEE

To my pastor and friend, Harry Walls

Thank you for the weeks you took to mentor me through Proverbs 7.
Your insights and wisdom are God-given genius.
Your treasuring of the glory of God is contagious. Your desire for the protection
and redemption of brothers in Christ from sexual sin is impassioning.
Your instruction and influence course deeply through this book. Indeed this book
never would have been without your time and investment in me.
Thank you for showing me how not to ruin my life.

Contents

Foreword

<u>SEX</u>. CAPITAL **S**, CAPITAL **E**, CAPITAL **X**.

Go ahead: say the word out loud. It's OK. Shout it from the top of your lungs. Don't be afraid. Sex is not a dirty word. Although our culture today has kidnapped this powerful word to mean something filthy and perverted, it's time for God's people to rescue it. Sex has never been our enemy. It hasn't ruined one single life on earth. It alone never has and never will. You might as well go ahead and get used to this word, if you're planning to make it past the first chapter of this book anyway. Personally, I love sex. It's actually by far the best wedding gift my wife and I received. I don't write any of this to be shocking or crude, but, in fact, to be the very opposite.

Sex is God's idea. Created by God for marriage between a man and a woman, and most of all, for His glory. Sex, submitted to biblical authority, is as pure as any other thing made by God. So go ahead…shout it out loud again. Even if you're young, old, single, or married, you don't have to flee from this word in order to find self-control. Love sex. God certainly does. Here is another word:

<u>SIN</u>. CAPITAL **S**, CAPITAL **I**, CAPITAL **N**.

Go ahead: say this word out loud as well. Shout it from the top of your lungs, but this time be afraid. Be very afraid. There is no dirtier word. Unlike sex, sin does nothing but ruin lives. Go ahead…shout it out loud again. Declare it an enemy and hate sin. God certainly does. One last word (well, maybe two!):

<u>SEXUAL SIN</u>. CAPITAL **R**, CAPITAL **U**, CAPITAL **I**, AND **N**.

Yes, when you put the words sex and sin together, you can always spell it as ruin: ruined lives, ruined marriages, ruined friendships, ruined reputations, ruined trust. In the following pages, my friend Jarrod Jones has done an amazing job of waging war against sexual sin. By using Proverbs 7 as a catalyst, Jarrod tackles this controversial topic in a biblically expository fashion. I love his honesty in these pages. Written from a ragamuffin's perspective, Jarrod uses his own failures and victories to connect with the reader. This is not a book written by a "know it all" who has conquered sinful temptation, but rather practical wisdom from a guy who has been there himself.

Whether you read this book as an individual or in a group setting, this book can save lives. As I was reading these chapters, I thought over and over again how I wish I had read this book when I was much younger. The pitfalls of sexual sin are just as real today as they have always been. A book like this can never be read soon enough by guys who desperately need to hear what God has to say on the topic of sex.

Having read Jarrod's writing in the past, and having heard him speak numerous times, I believe this is his best work yet. Thanks, Jarrod, for writing such a needed book about such a neglected topic. Sure, there are other books about battling sexual sin, but none that I have read as practical and simply put for men, whether single, married, young, or old.

—David Nasser
Internationally known speaker and author of
Glory Revealed; A Call to Grace; and *A Call to Die.*

Introduction

13 WAYS TO RUIN YOUR LIFE
A PRACTICAL GUIDE FOR GUYS

I was 13 years old. Baseball and friends were my passion. I was a fairly good kid except for the occasional cursing, dipping Skoal˚, and toking on a cigarette.

Girls were mysterious and intimidating. I was scared to death of the species. I ignored them mostly because any attention I gave them, or that they gave me, made my face glow sunburn red.

Things began to change in the seventh grade. I sat behind a certain girl in history class. Before each class, she would turn around and try to talk to me. But I'd lean over, not wanting her to see my face shine, wrap an arm around my notebook, draw it close to me as if gathering poker chips, then bury my pen and face into the page writing in a nervous fury. She would laugh; thought it was cute, I guess. All semester she talked to me and I began to feel more and more at ease. Then one day she pushed her chips all in: "If I gave you the chance, would you have sex with me?" I was horrified, but strangely moved. I said "yeah" because that's what cool guys say. Nothing ever came of it though. But I always wondered, *what if?* I never forgot her question. I've never forgotten the magical way the word "sexxx" hissed off of her tongue.

The spring semester ended and summer began. Early in the summer a friend and I were walking along railroad tracks in my former hometown of Clanton, Alabama. We were kicking around rocks, balancing on the tracks as if on high beams, cursing, and chewing tobacco. We happened upon a magazine at the bottom of a bridge. Someone must have thrown it out of their car a few days before because the pages were thick, torn in places, and folded. I picked up the magazine, thumbing through it while jabbing with my buddy.

It was a *Hustler* porn magazine. What I held before me branded itself into my mind. I can still see those images today. I sat down on the rail and dissected every page. My friend hovered over me as we "whooooaaa-ed."

I was captivated. It became my most prized possession. I nearly enshrined it. I studied it daily, as if cramming for a final exam. Fantasies were born. I hid it in drawers under my clothing.

One day I came home after carpet cleaners had been at our house. I found the magazine laying on top of my desk in all its glory. I choked back the vomit thinking that my mom had seen it. Embarrassed to the marrow, I threw it away.

In the months that followed I regretted that I had thrown it away. I missed it like an addiction. I was in withdrawal. I needed a fix. I was consumed with finagling a way to get another porn magazine. Sometimes I got more than I bargained for. Friends introduced me to their dad's video porn collection. Porn had me by the throat.

One fact I've learned as I reflect on being a youngster exposed to the power of porn: I didn't have to go looking for it; it came looking for me. Porn, and past images from encounters with it, haunt me, hunt me, and beckon me in various degrees, forms, and moments. I wonder if you deal with the same.

What I have learned from Scripture, observation, and from "close-call" sexual experiences as a college student and single adult, is that sexual immorality is a life-ruiner. I'm including pornography in the definition of sexual immorality. Jesus would too.

Pornography consists of the joining of two Greek words: *porneia* and *grapho*. In the gospel of Matthew (Matthew 5:32), Jesus used the Greek word *porneia*. It is a broad term that encompasses every form of sexual immorality, not just adultery. It includes homosexuality, bestiality, heterosexual pre-marital sex, oral sex, anal sex, sexual petting, lust, and so forth. *Porenia* is where we get the English phrase "porn" or "porno." The Greek word *grapho* is where we get porn*ography*. *Grapho* means "to write or draw." Pornography therefore is sexual immorality in a graphic, picture form.

Though *porneia* is a broad term including all sexual immorality, someone might make the case that the context of Jesus' use of *porneia* in Matthew 5 was in the context of only adultery. Still, according to Jesus in Matthew 5:28, lust is equal to committing adultery. And pornography is lust-driven.

Bank on the fact that sexual immorality will ruin your life. It will destroy you and everything you know and love. If you are in a fight to the death with this terrorist, this book is going to give you 13 ways of how to lose the fight. If you buy into and follow these 13 ways, I'd bet "all-in" that your life and relationships as you know them will be shattered.

On a positive note, however, there is hope. I believe that you can gain more and more victory over sexual immorality by running opposite the 13 ways presented in this book and following the plethora of Scriptures that counter them.

This book is written for Christian men: old, young-ish, single or married. But if you're a man outside the faith who has happened upon this book, I hope you will read it too. The truths are timeless and can be applied no matter where you are in life.

My ultimate hope, however, is that you would first come to saving faith in Jesus Christ. Only Christ will satisfy your deepest yearnings. Salvation in Christ comes by believing with all of your mind and heart that Jesus was both God and man, born through the Virgin Mary, lived a sinless life, died on the cross for your sins while taking God's holy wrath upon Himself, resurrected the third day conquering sin and death, now reigns in heaven, and is coming again as the Warrior, King, and Judge. Crucial to your belief is that you confess (agree with God) that you're a sinner, receive His forgiveness, and repent (turn away from) of the sin in your life. In so doing, Jesus is your Savior, and your *Lord*. With Jesus as your Lord, you obey Him with your life. One of the key areas, as presented in this book, is obeying Him with your sexual life. To do so glorifies Him (which, in turn, satisfies you), and protects you from ruin.

The following 13 ways plucked from Proverbs 7 are all it takes to be thrown onto the horns of ruin. Run from the ways and you'll live. Follow the ways and you're doomed.

How To Ruin Your Life in 13 Ways
PROVERBS 7

1 *Follow my advice, my son; always treasure my commands.*
2 *Obey my commands and live! Guard my instructions as you guard your own eyes.*
3 *Tie them on your fingers as a reminder. Write them deep within your heart.*
4 *Love wisdom like a sister; make insight a beloved member of your family.*
5 *Let them protect you from an affair with an immoral woman,*
from listening to the flattery of a promiscuous woman.
6 *While I was at the window of my house, looking through the curtain,*
7 *I saw some naive young men, and one in particular who lacked common sense.*
8 *He was crossing the street near the house of an immoral woman, strolling down*
the path by her house. 9 *It was at twilight, in the evening, as deep darkness fell.*
10 *The woman approached him, seductively dressed and sly of heart.*
11 *She was the brash, rebellious type, never content to stay at home.*
12 *She is often in the streets and markets, soliciting at every corner.*
13 *She threw her arms around him and kissed him, and with a brazen look she*
said, 14 *"I've just made my peace offerings and fulfilled my vows.* 15 *You're the one*
I was looking for! I came out to find you, and here you are! 16 *My bed is spread*
with beautiful blankets, with colored sheets of Egyptian linen. 17 *I've perfumed*
my bed with myrrh, aloes, and cinnamon. 18 *Come, let's drink our fill*
of love until morning. Let's enjoy each other's caresses, 19 *for my husband*
is not home. He's away on a long trip. 20 *He has taken a wallet full*
of money with him and won't return until later this month."
21 *So she seduced him with her pretty speech and enticed him with her flattery.*
22 *He followed her at once, like an ox going to the slaughter. He was like a stag*
caught in a trap, 23 *awaiting the arrow that would pierce its heart. He was like*
a bird flying into a snare, little knowing it would cost him his life.
24 *So listen to me, my sons, and pay attention to my words.*
25 *Don't let your hearts stray away toward her. Don't wander down*
her wayward path. 26 *For she has been the ruin of many;*
many men have been her victims. 27 *Her house is the road to the grave.*
Her bedroom is the den of death.

TIP #1

BE UNRESOLVED

And I saw among the naïve,
And discerned among the youths,
A young man lacking sense.

- PROVERBS 7:7

It was August 1997. I was wrestling with the decision of going to graduate school in order to be either a high school teacher or a pastor. I spoke with the pastor of my church at the time. He told me not to expect a parting of the heavens and an angel descending with a scroll revealing God's direction in my life. He said, "If you go into the ministry, 'stick a proverbial flag in the ground' and don't look back. There will come tough times when you'll doubt if you made the right decision. And it's then you'll reflect back to see that flag as the place and time you declared your commitment to God. No matter how hard life and ministry get, that flag is a declaration of your commitment."

TENACIOUS RESOLVE

Resolve. It's sticking the flag into the soil of your heart and not looking back. It's driving home a vow to God to stay committed to your intended purpose.

It's fighting for it with all your might no matter what temptations come. It's having moments of heavy temptation yet remembering your commitment to God for mental and physical purity. In life there are always situations and moments where we fail in our commitments to others, to ourselves, and to Christ. Yet the beauty of having this "flag in the soil" is that it gives us a marker to come back to when we feel like we've strayed from God's purpose. Sexual sin is no different. If God has convicted your heart and there is a discomfort in your soul about sexual sin in your life, you must repent and reconcile with Him. The easiest way to lose the fight against sexual sin is to simply ignore or deny the sin and be unresolved in dealing with it.

In Proverbs 7, Solomon is displaying the lack of resolve of the young man. The young man has no flag driven into the ground. He's curious. He's passive. He's open to sexual sin. He's seducible. He thinks he can just check her out, maybe make out, have a night out, then a night in, and move on with his life. He's naïve. We can be just as naïve. Think about this in the context of porn: *Just a quick glance and it will never happen again.*

On the other hand, resolve is commitment, discipline, maturity, wisdom, discernment, and devotion. Resolve is a doggedness to seek God in your life and to obey Him with your life. It's a tenacity to be righteous—right with God and others, and living right before God and others, for the glory of God. That is what the flag of righteousness looks like. It's the righteousness of heart and mind.

LOST RESOLVE

I was single for 31 years. Around 23 years old, I was in a committed relationship with a girl I thought I would marry. I confess I'd been sexually active in my younger years. But I wanted to save myself for her. I wanted our first time together sexually to be perfect. I considered "perfect" to involve wedding rings on our fingers, vows made before God and family, and a gloriously intimate first night. I had made sexual mistakes in the past. But I refused to allow this relationship to become tainted, poisoned if you will, with sexual sin. I resolved to keep our relationship sexually pure.

Over time my resolve weakened. It didn't help that *she* wanted to get more "intimate" (which was a first for me). So I began rationalizing: *We're getting married one day anyway.* I didn't hold to my resolve. Too many late nights alone with her, too much snuggling, too much pushing of sexual boundaries. Then one night after a movie, alone in my apartment, we had sex. That moment did what I knew it would do. It changed everything. I felt guilty and she felt guilty. This is one of the sexual consequences I had hoped to avoid for the rest of my life. Still my resolve lessened even more. The guilt would last only about an hour.

The center of our relationship became sex. I became "addicted" to her. In other words, she was all I could think about. We had crossed over the sexual line. As a result, jealousy over her, control of her, suspicion about her with other guys, and constant panic about our relationship haunted me. Our relationship was doomed because of that night months before when I became unresolved.

The inevitable happened. She left me for another guy weeks before I was going to propose to her. My soul felt ripped apart. I couldn't sleep. I couldn't eat. I couldn't quit crying. The heartfelt pain was ruthless. I'd rather have been tortured physically than go through such pain emotionally. Granted, not every guy handles the fallout as I did when a relationship centered on sex ends. But the emotional and relational trauma of a sexual relationship gone bust happens to many guys though we try to "man up" and never admit it. Perhaps you can relate. I should have known that becoming unresolved sexually would lead to devastation. But somehow, I didn't see it coming.

RESTORED RESLOVE

I felt the jagged edges of a broken heart for months, even years. In that brokenness the Lord drew me to Himself. Like the beat-down, lonely, broken, prodigal son returning home to the love and warmth of His father, so I embraced the Father and repented of sexual sin. The Lord put men, young and old, into my life to encourage me to pursue Jesus over everything and everyone else. I grew closer and deeper in relationship with Jesus. I found

Him to be my loving Savior and satisfier. He filled the void in my life that I had been trying to fill by an intimate relationship with a girl. Meanwhile, two markers became as true as air to me: 1) I never wanted to go through that emotional pain again; 2) I never wanted to be "separated" from the Father again. But that would happen only by driving the flag of resolve deep into my soul.

Sexual temptation still ebbed and flowed in various ways and intensity. And it isn't as if I'm immune now. Nevertheless, I vowed a renewed and resolved virginity. I'm proud to say that before I met Christie, the woman who would become my wife, I had remained sexually pure (physically and visually) for seven years. Believe me, the resolve was well worth the long wait.

FUTURE SEX

As a single man during those seven years, it was hardcore remaining sexually pure in mind and body. *If only I was married,* I thought, *then sexual temptation wouldn't be so intense.* I had this idea that marriage was a cure for the sin of lust. I thought wives and husbands had sex every day of the workweek, after quiet time devotions at night, and even walked around the house naked all day on weekends. Physical intimacy with my wife would happen whenever the urge struck me. Wrong.

I was a bit narrow-minded. Marriage is not about sex. If you're not married, fellas, let me go ahead and spoil a couple of surprises for you: There isn't sex everyday. And married people don't walk around the house naked on weekends because that would be . . . weird. But don't get me wrong. Marriage is great and physical intimacy is fabulous! It's a gift from God. But physical intimacy is *not* the center of a marriage.

Physical intimacy is not just a physical act either. It's more. It's emotional, and spiritual. The physical act is never enough. It never satisfies. In the covenant of marriage, where God intends physical intimacy, a sense of fulfillment is found when bodies and beings are engaged as "one." I will admit that although physical intimacy with my wife helps with lust, it doesn't help completely. Marriage is not a cure-all for lust.

THE MANTRA

It was a pretty big deal for me to come to terms with the above truth. I'd spent seven years believing the opposite. But in accepting the reality that marriage *isn't* a cure-all for lust, I developed a mantra that I live by to this day. When sexual temptation taps into my mind or catches my eye, I literally say out loud: *"Lust will never satisfy."*

This mantra, this truth, kept to the front of the mind and heart, is a simple, biblical, and powerful weapon. Lust does not and will never satisfy. Think about it. No matter how soft the porn or hard-core perverse the porn, your craving will never be quenched. In addition, she may be "smokin' hot" but there will always be another girl who is "hotter." You can look the girl up and down and fantasize all day and night about what you would do with her sexually, but you can never stare and fantasize until your heart's content and your sexual craving is satisfied. Lust cannot content a heart.

Furthermore, no matter with whom you have sex, how many women you have sex with, or how much sex you have, you will find yourself emptier and emptier, and needing more and more. You will never be satisfied . . . ever.

THE FLAG

So how do we create these "flags" in our own lives? King David penned a psalm that was his flag in the ground to be right with God and live right before God. Sense the intense resolve in King David's words. "I will walk within my house in the integrity of my heart. I will set no worthless thing before my eyes; I hate the work of those who fall away; It shall not fasten its grip on me. A perverse heart shall depart from me; I will know no evil."[1]

Notice the "*I will*" and the "*it shall . . .*". This is resolve. This is a flag driven into the ground to deny sexual immorality. It's a declaration to walk in purity. Will you be this resolved?

According to Scripure, to be unresolved means to be "naïve" and "lacking sense."[2] In the words of my pastor, it means you are "open-doored" or open-minded when it comes to sexual temptation and situations. There are some things God calls you to have the door closed on in your life. According to Proverbs 5, 6, 7, and many other texts, sexual immorality is number one.

Resolve to be righteous. Take the flag of sexual "rightness" before God and drive it into the soil of your heart. Take some time and get away. Spend time alone with God in the Word and prayer. Plead for grace to be resolved and righteous. Then drive the flag into the ground. When sexual temptation is screaming at you or lurking within you, stop, reflect on the flag, and watch it flapping in the wind. And say, "Right there in that place I resolved to die to my lusts, submit my sexual temptations before the cross, and surrender my sexual sin to Christ. I am resolved."

Be resolved to not be ruined.

INVENTORY

◆ Will you resolve in the private places of your life, business, cubicle, home, college dorm, etc. to walk in integrity of heart and mind?

◆ Will you resolve to put no worthless thing before your eyes by way of Internet, cable TV, DVDs, magazines, and so forth? How?

◆ Will you resolve to prayerfully develop a sacred fear and hatred of sexual sin and that which seduces you toward it? How will you pray?

◆ Will you resolve to do whatever it takes to keep sexual immorality from fastening its grip on you? What actions can you take?

◆ Will you resolve to purge perversity from your heart and mind? How can it be purged?

◆ Will you resolve in advance what you will do when sexual opportunities in all forms come? If so, what are some things you can do?

◆ Memorize Psalm 101:2-4 and claim it in times of temptation.

TIP #2

FLIRT WITH TEMPTATION

He was going down the street near her corner,
walking along in the direction of her house
at twilight, as the day was fading,
as the dark of night set in.

- PROVERBS 7:8

Before basketball season my junior year at Samford, I brought one of my teammates home with me for my mom's homecooking. It was Sunday afternoon. We were in the front yard tossing the football. We happened across a certain hole in the ground while running pass routes. My friend Brad, my dad, and I circled the hole, squatted down, and eye-balled it trying to figure out what might be lurking within.

As soon as Dad said, "It's a yellow jacket nest," a yellow jacket buzzed from behind us and came in for a slow landing on the rim of the hole. Then it calmly crawled in. With grins, Brad and I looked at each other as if we'd read each other's minds. We got a big mason jar from my mom and stood it upside down over the hole. We stomped the ground around the hole as hard as we could. Like water out of a hose, yellow jackets sprayed into the jar, filling the jar, and pinging the glass in a fury. Dad was leaning over the jar and

Brad snuck up behind him, pinched him on the back of the leg, and went "Bzzzt!" Dad yelped and leaped three feet off the ground. Little did we know that the joke would soon be on us.

It was surreal. In slow motion the jar tipped over a smidge, teetered on its edge for a teasing moment, and fell. We were frozen in unbelief. It felt like a cartoon. It was as if the yellow jackets raised their stingers to full mast, cocked back, and exploded after us in a wailing rage.

We screamed and ran for our lives. I went in one direction, Brad went in another, and my dad disappeared all together. Dad somehow made it to the other side of the house. Brad was still tearing through the yard doing some two-step gallop thing and howling. I, on the other hand, ended up on the front porch swatting, swinging, shrieking, spitting, and trying to hold my bowels. From there everything else is a blur. All said and done, my dad escaped, my teammate took a hit in the back of the leg, and I took one in the back shoulder. Sweet memories. . . .

That's what can happen when you flirt around with sexual sin too. You might get away with it for a while. You can get comfortable, secure, and think you've got it under control. You think you've got it nailed. The fact of the matter is that you're the one about to get nailed, or rather "stung." Flirting with temptation can lead to pain, humiliation, regret, and disaster.

THE MENU MENTALITY

I've heard men, even Christian men, say, while staring at an attractive woman, "I can look at the menu as long as I don't order from it." This is deception and ignorance. When I look at restaurant menus and a dinner grabs my eye, I start thinking about it arriving on the plate, how it delicious it will smell, and the taste that will amaze me. Looking at women as if they are "menus" takes you down the same path. Sexually speaking, that path is called lust. And if you look at the menu long enough, eventually you will eat.

I'm a big believer that "innocent" looks, remarks, playful conversations, and so forth can lead to bigger issues, such as emotional attachments, sexual connotations, sexual surrender, wrecked relationships, and ultimately a ruined life. But it's intriguing how we rationalize sexual temptation. We set ourselves up for the fall when we give ourselves permission just to take a peak, or say "hello," or sit closer, stare longer, or stand nearer. Singles live on the razor thin edge of *how far is too far?* As a teenager and a single man until 31 years old, I know I did.

So how far is too far? In Romans 13:14, the apostle Paul states, "But put on the Lord Jesus Christ, and make no provision for the flesh, to fulfill its lusts."[1] In other words, if you make provision for lust, you will be intensely moved to satisfy your lusts. Don't go there.

Paul also states, "[A]mong you there must not be even a hint of sexual immorality, or of any kind of impurity . . .".[2] Put yourself in a bad position and you will go too far. Acually, anything that smacks of sexual sin is already too far. There is more discussion on this and Scripture-based dating standards later in the book.

For now, how do you keep yourself out of the *how far is too far* situations? Again, the apostle Paul: "So put to death the sinful, earthly things lurking within you. Have nothing to do with sexual sin, impurity, lust and shameful desires."[3] In other words, the very question of *how far is too far* and the statement, "just looking at the menu and not ordering from it," shouldn't even be in your vocabulary. Kill that rationale. It's a non-issue, a closed door.

My pastor stated it this way, "It's not if but when." It's not if you'll go too far, but when you'll go too far. It's not if you'll get ruined, but when you'll get ruined.

EMOTIONAL ADULTERY

On another note, getting involved with a dinner menu doesn't normally engage your emotions. Because you think you've detached from women sexually doesn't mean you stay detached emotionally. Flirting with women can lead to disaster. Emotions can get triggered. What starts out as an innocent remark and flattery can morph into much pain and regret.

When I was a 28-year old single, seminary student, I met an older gentleman in his mid- to late-60s. He was pastor and a licensed professional counselor. I met with him periodically to discuss areas of struggle. One day we were dealing with how sexual pasts can scar and hinder healthy relationships with women. He shared with me something shocking. It was something I had never heard of or even considered. Many years prior to our meeting, a flirtatious relationship developed between him and a church secretary at a previous church he'd pastored. It never became a physical relationship, he said. Emotionally, however, he became deeply attached to her. And the emotions continued escalating. He fought it and fought it. It became so intense that he decided to share his "emotional adultery" (what he called it) with his wife. His wife considered it emotional *adultery* too. She divorced him a year later.

I'll never forget the regret in his eyes. I learned something I'd never before considered: emotions are nothing to play around with; they are nuclear.

If you're single, you are emotionally vulnerable. Just last night I hung out with three single friends of mine who struggle with what I struggled with as a single man years ago: the longing for companionship, the weariness of loneliness. Sexual temptation sometimes is not the biggest factor. It's the desire for a companion, a longing to connect deeply and emotionally. However, emotional engagement with a woman can quickly overwhelm rationale. It can put you on a romantic high that sets you up for disaster. An emotionally charged and ruled relationship with a woman can lead to heartbreak, impulsive decisions, and potentially sexual ruin. Be careful with your emotions. Embrace and express them wisely.

For a married man, emotional connections are for your wife only and no other. An emotional attachment with another woman leads to emotional disengagement from your wife. This is dangerous territory because doubts can birth about your marriage. Fantasies can arise about the relationship possibilities with the other woman. Emotional bonding can lead to sexual sin. Or at the least, like my pastor friend, it falls into emotional adultery. Emotional adultery means that your emotions, which were to be protected and nurtured for your wife only, are allowed to run freely with another woman. Keep a reign on your emotions. Beware of emotional adultery. It can ruin you.

CHRISTIAN SEX

Sexual rationalization among teenagers and singles, as well as young and old singles, can become biblically irrational and sinful. There is an actual term coined "Christian sex." According to a teenage guy I spoke with a year ago, Christian sex is anything but sexual intercourse. Sexual petting, mutual masturbation, anal sex, and oral sex are okay because there has been no actual "sex," he argued. I just read a blog yesterday from a gal who argued the same thing. So they can still call themselves virgins and avoid guilt. They are deceived that purity only applies to sexual intercourse. As a teenager and young single guy, I used this rationalization too, albeit I didn't use those exact terms. And looking back, there was still guilt. Nonetheless, there is only one kind of "Christian sex" the Bible endorses and celebrates—marital sex.

Remember Jesus' use of *porneia* in the gospel of Matthew (see introduction chapter). It's a wide term that defines sexual sin—sexual activity outside of marriage. It includes oral sex, anal sex, mutual masturbation, "dry humping," and any other kind of sexual petting—what my friend and other Christian young men and women have called "Christian sex." The Bible does paint a beautiful picture of Christian sex, but sex outside of God's will isn't it. In fact, Jesus uses two other words in place of what others have called "Christian sex." He calls it "sexual sin"—*porneia.*

Pushing sexual boundaries and justifying how far you can go sexually veers you further from purity and headlong into *porneia.* Shouldn't this matter to a Christ-follower? According to the Scriptures, a Christian man wants of himself what Christ desires of him—purity. In turn, he prays and takes steps to pursue it. How far can I *get* from *porneia* and how far can I *go* to have *purity* is the *how far is too far* question that a Christ-follower should be asking.

God champions romance and physical intimacy but only within marriage. Sexual freedom and pleasure experienced in the souls of husband and wife is incredible. It's a gift that's hard to describe. King Solomon gets close though. In the book Song of Songs, King Solomon pens poetic metaphors and vivid imagery to express sexual bliss in marriage. The following is a portrait of Christian sex:

[The young man declares:] Oh how delightful you are, my beloved; how pleasant for utter delight! [Y]our breasts are like clusters of dates. I said, 'I will climb up into the palm tree and take hold of its branches.' Now may your breasts be like grape clusters, and the scent of your breath like apples. May your kisses be as exciting as the best wine, smooth and sweet, flowing gently over lips and teeth. [The young woman responds:] I am my lover's, the one he desires. Come, my love, let us go out into the fields and spend the night among the wildflowers. Let us get up early and go out to the vineyards. . . . And there I will give you my love.[4]

This is not just any sexual encounter. This is an exciting sexual encounter between husband and wife. This is physical intimacy as God intended it to be. Romantic, fulfilling, exciting, freeing, satisfying, God-glorifying. Also in the book of Song of Songs God grants sexual freedom between husband and wife. In other words, if husband and wife are willing to explore each other's bodies sexually outside of intercourse, and neither feel degraded in ways of doing so, there is a green light.[5] As Mark Driscoll, pastor of Mars Hill Church, Seattle Washington, shared (to the best of my memory), it's not as if Jesus is standing there with a ref's jersey and a whistle calling foul. God made husband and wife to enjoy each other sexually as "one."[6] It all fits within the oneness of the marriage covenant. So enjoy! There is no fear of consequences or ruin. Christian sex!

MASTURBATION

What about masturbation? Is it exempt? Can masturbation be a method to deter Christian men from sexual sin? Or is it sexual sin? It's hard to imagine masturbation without pornographic imagery, or mental fantasy, and lust. If that's the case, we've already understood what Jesus said about lust. It's sin. It's not as if a man can masturbate while thinking about raking leaves. It's not the act of masturbation that is sinful but the *lust* that drives the act. It's lust and that which fuels the lust that must be targeted, not the act. As the lust—along with the sinful passions and desires—is targeted with prayer, Scripture, repentance, accountability, and faith in Christ to deliver, the act by default is targeted too. Victory over masturbation comes and goes in parallel with the victory over lust. Lust is the greater issue because it can lead to more than masturbation. It can lead to ruin.

However, many men believe the urge to act on lust through masturbation is far too great to resist. Can this really be true for Christians? We've been given the Spirit of Jesus. He has called us and empowered us by His Spirit to crucify our flesh "with its passions and desires" and not submit to them.[7] Nowhere in Scripture do you find permission for someone to surrender to strong passions and desires that are of the flesh. Instead you will find the command (and thankfully for us, the power) to crucify it.

The Spirit of God has called and empowered us by His Spirit to a life of self-control.[8] The apostle Paul says,

> Do not let sin control the way you live; do not give in to its lustful desires. Do not let any part of your body become a tool of wickedness, to be used for sinning. Instead, give yourselves completely to God since you have been given new life. And use your whole body as a tool to do what is right for the glory of God. Sin is no longer your master . . .".[9]

Paul adds this declaration later: "I urge you, in view of God's mercy, to offer your bodies as living sacrifices, holy and pleasing to God—this is your spiritual act of worship."[10] I find strength and perspective here. Paul prefaces his plea with "in view of God's mercy." He's not inspiring us, cheering us on, "rah-rah-ing" us on to holiness. No, he's pointing us to what will give us victory—keeping our eyes on God's mercy. God's mercy was displayed in Jesus taking our sin on the cross. The cross of Christ is where we constantly see God's unconditional love for us, we who were and are grossly unworthy of His love. It's His mercy that motivates, not our self-motivation. This is not legalism. It's His grace and love that moves us to set our bodies apart for His glory and for our good.

Sex outside of marriage can be rationalized or "Christianized" all day but it doesn't make it Christian. Whatever label is attached to "sex" outside of marriage, it cannot be pressed or debated into the conscience that desires to honor Christ. Again, there is only one kind of "Christian sex" that honors Christ, and only one the Scriptures endorse and celebrate: marital sex.

So what can we take away from all that we've discussed about flirting with temptation? According to my experience, you don't mess around with yellow jackets. They will nail you. According to God's truth, you don't flirt around with sexual sin; it can ruin you.

So run for your life.

INVENTORY

◆ What are the triggers of sexual temptation in your life?

◆ What boundaries do you need to set in your life not only to protect you from sexual sin, but also to prevent you from even flirting with it?

◆ As a single man or a married man, what do you believe you need to avoid when spending time with a woman not your wife? How careful will you resolve to be?

◆ What sexual opportunities are easy to flirt with in life? What opportunities are you flirting with?

◆ Do you have the attitude of *I'm just looking at the menu, not ordering from it?* Do you rationalize and toe the line with *how far is too far?* What's the danger here?

◆ How do you crucify your flesh "with its passions and desires"?

TIP #3

FEEL YOU'RE IN CONTROL

She is often seen in the streets and markets, soliciting at every corner.

- PROVERBS 7:12

Don't let your heart stray toward her. Don't wander down her wayward path.

- PROVERBS 7:25

Timothy Treadwell was an avid outdoorsman and photographer of grizzly bears. Archived video footage shows Treadwell "often within arm's reach of large brown bears, or creeping on all fours toward a sow and her three cubs, talking in a soft sing-song voice."[1] Convinced he was safe and in control, Treadwell became more and more daring. He no longer saw danger. But in October 2003, Timothy Treadwell and his girlfriend, Amie Huguenard, were mauled and eaten by a grizzly bear. Writer Kevin Sanders shares the story:

On Monday October 6, 2003 sometime in the afternoon, air taxi pilot Willy Hall from Andrew Airways arrives to transport Tim and Amie out of the area for the year, and is charged by a large, but skinny and ill kept brown bear. The pilot then takes off and flies over the campsite in an attempt to chase the bear away and sees what appears to be a large bear on a human body.

On Wednesday October 8, 2003, park rangers and Alaska State Troopers arrive and shoot a large brown bear when it charges them, then later kill a second smaller, younger bear after it approaches them while they are loading the remains in the plane, and later discover the now infamous six minutes of tape.

The first sounds from the tape are from Amie, "she sounds surprised and asks if it's still out there". The next voice is from Timothy as he screams "Get out of here; the bear is killing me!" (It appears that Tim was wearing a remote microphone on his coveralls.) Amie then yells over the background sounds of the bear and Timothy fighting to "play dead!", then "fight it!", Timothy then screams, and yells at Amie to "hit the bear with a pan," "you have to hit the bear!" The tape then runs out and stops . . . . [2]

Common sense says you don't tempt bears. You can't control a bear. Treadwell had the illusion that he could. He lost his life. Similarly the "feeling" that you're in control of sexual temptation or sexual sin is a delusion.

THE PREDATOR

Satan, through sexual temptations and immorality, is a predator. Predators prowl around, hunt you down, and eat you. You can't control predators. "[The devil] prowls around like a roaring lion, looking for some victim to devour."[3]

Satan, through sexual sin and immorality, is also like a terrorist. Terrorists take you off guard. They watch for your most vulnerable moment and then attack. You don't have to go looking for terrorists. They're coming after you. A terrorist has one goal in mind: to destroy you. You can't control a terrorist. "Be careful! Watch out for attacks from the devil, your great enemy." [4]

Satan is the aggressor and mastermind behind the immorality and he can attack in different ways. For instance, he can attack you sneakily and unexpectedly. You'll never see it coming.

SNEAK ATTACK

When I was in high school, my godly grandmother visited us on a Sunday afternoon. Mom was putting the finishing touches on lunch while we sat in the living room watching television. This was back in the day when we had the mega-satellite dish that took up a quarter of the backyard. That thing looked like we were trying to contact someone out in the Milky Way.

To get a particular channel through the satellite you would have to punch the channel number into the remote and then hit a button that would swing the satellite around into another direction. In the process of the satellite dish creaking its way around to the direction needed, it would briefly pick up other cable programs. The programs would slowly fade in, sit for a few seconds, then fade out. Needless to say, programs for which we had no subscription or access would be scanned over.

On this particular Sunday, Dad flipped on the television to pass the time. He punched in the info to take us to another channel, a football game most likely. What happened next was like an out-of-body experience.

The satellite dish slowly made its turn. Appearing into view was a channel I didn't know existed with our satellite capability. In faded a woman and man in full-throttle, full-view, explicit sex. Sound effects included.

In stunned silence I sat beside my sweet and saintly grandmother as the porn scene slowly, ever so painfully slowly, unfolded. I pleaded for Jesus' return, or my death, whichever might come first.

I was suspended between hell and earth. It took an eternity for that channel to fade out of view. There was nothing I, or Dad, could do. He couldn't have reversed the direction of the dish or it would have stopped in the middle of the scene before reversing to the previous channel. In other words, it would have remained there longer. I could have walked out of the room I suppose. But that would have required bodily function, of which I had none.

As the channel mercifully faded out of view we sat in an eerie silence. I cut my eyes over at my grandmother. She showed no emotion. Oddly, her expression never changed. I looked over at Dad. He sat pale and frozen. Then he looked at me, cleared his throat and said, "Well, what's for lunch?"

I never would have dreamed of a "sexual attack" in front of my grandmother. That even sounds gross. But the enemy approached sneakily and unexpectedly. Then he attacked violently. It mattered not who was around at the time. He was on a mission.

His aggression paid off. Guess what I did the next time I was home alone? I tried to find that channel. It wasn't hard to find. Even in that humiliating moment around my family, I had memorized how and where to locate that program. I nearly worked the satellite dish off its hinges for weeks as I went back and forth to that channel. The enemy's mission was accomplished, at least for a time.

FRONTAL ASSAULT

Another way the attack comes is openly and aggressively. You can see it coming a mile away. These are powerful attacks.

Christie and I were engaged for ten months. Once a month I would fly to Hartford, Connecticut from Louisville, Kentucky to visit her. From Hartford to Wilton, Connecticut was about an hour and thirty minutes drive. In December 2002, my plane landed in Hartford in the midst of a snowstorm. Christie barely made it to the airport because the roads were icy. Once I got my baggage we were in the car and off to Wilton. The problem, however, was the police started closing the roads. We still had an option to drive on to Wilton but the roads were so iced over the car was fishtailing.

We decided we had to splurge on hotel rooms for the night. After checking two to three hotels, the only hotel room left was at a Super 8. Notice I said hotel room, not rooms. We had no choice. I booked the one hotel room.

We knew the sexual opportunity that stood before us. It was no secret the temptation that awaited us. Thankfully the room had twin beds. I made a call to a buddy. I told him the situation. I asked him to pray against temptation for us. Then I gave him permission to ask me the hard questions the next day. We slept in different beds and left early morning the next day. We didn't even hold hands.

There was no control over the situation that night. I had no control over the weather. I saw the sexual enemy in plain sight. I knew what was coming. I knew what he was up to. I was aware of his schemes.[5] I wasn't stupid enough to believe I had control over the sexual possibilities between Christie and me that night. My buddy prayed for us. I prayed silently as I checked us into our room. I'm sure Christie prayed. But Christie and I didn't pray together. I remembered a friend telling me that he thinks more sexual encounters happen between a Christian guy and girl praying together than at other times. I don't know where he got his facts but I wasn't taking any chances.

SEXUAL AGGRESSION AND ACCESS

Sexual sin comes aggressively. Solomon uses the immoral woman to reveal this truth. He says she "seeks him, comes out to meet him, kisses him, persuades him, flatters him, and seduces him."[6] She's aggressive. She's doing this in public. Immorality sometimes just reveals itself in all its glory, doesn't it? And interesting how often we can find ourselves more impacted by this than the unexpected temptation. The flat-out immorality can tap into our carnal nature and awaken lust.

Immorality is also accessible and available. Solomon adds that the woman is "often seen in the streets and markets, soliciting at every corner."[7] You don't have to go looking for immorality on the city street downtown, or on the Internet, or at the beach on spring break. It lurks within the very relationships around you. The enemy comes after you in the relationship with your girlfriend or fiancé that you've committed to purity before God. He prowls around in the youth ministry, your small group, and your church congregation.

STAYING THE DISTANCE

The enemy behind the sexual temptation and immorality must not be taken lightly. After reading the Treadwell story, you wouldn't take a grizzly bear lightly, would you? I went to Alaska to speak at a conference not long ago. As I exited the plane in Anchorage, there in the lobby stood an encased grizzly bear. I have never seen anything that huge and ferocious up close. Believe me, I would never dream of getting cozy and comfortable with a freak of nature like that. And neither would you. You would avoid it completely or keep your distance at all costs. Similarly, after reading Solomon's story of the young man in Proverbs 7, you should avoid sexual temptation at all costs. On the other hand, although you can't completely avoid all avenues of sexual temptation, you can labor at keeping your distance. Pointers on how you can practically do this are found in the pages to come.

Nevertheless, sexual immorality is aggressive, accessible, available, and even appealing. You have to anticipate sexual temptations at every turn in your life. Not fear it, anticipate it. My pastor made a great point. He said you don't go into every sales venture thinking that the salesperson is going to be completely objective and up-front with you. Most likely he or she is going to make the item over-appealing. The salesperson is going to highlight the bells and whistles of it. We'd be foolish walking into any place not anticipating this. The negative has to be anticipated, or we could make a purchase that costs way more than we intended to pay.

The same goes for sexual temptation. Anticipate the highlights and appeal of sexual temptations that will be presented around you and before you wherever you go. Ready yourself with the reality that the temptation is going to look irresistible and incredible. Expect your senses to be assaulted in a sneak attack or frontal assault. Be ready to run, not rationalize. Be prepared to turn away from and not buy into. To do otherwise can cost you royally.

I'm sure that earlier in Treadwell's adventures he anticipated danger and was more cautious in dealing with bears. But over time he became deceived and hardened, and no longer anticipated danger. He felt he was in control. Little did he know that befriending bears would destroy him and the one he loved.

911

The enemy, through immorality, is a predator. He can bring about seemingly irresistible sexual opportunities. He can bombard you with overwhelming sexual temptation. You don't have to go looking for it. It comes to you. When it happens don't try to conquer and control. Get out of there. A way out is promised and provided. Read what the Bible has to say about this. This is a big deal: "And God is faithful. He will keep the temptation from becoming so strong that you can't stand up against it. When you are tempted, he will show you a way out so that you will not give in to it."[8] Keep in mind, this Scripture is to be called on as a way of life and not just before you take your pants off.

There is a notion among some Chrisitan men that the way they can finally defeat their sin is by willingly placing themselves in the very temptations that had been defeating them. It appeals to the "warrior" in us. If we defeat the temptation then we can declare victory over our sin. For example, say a guy is battling with a habit of looking at pornography on the Internet. He comes to the end of himself, again, and decides he will prove to himself and God that he will beat his sin. So late one night he walks into his room and goes to the "click here to enter" page for a showdown with the sin. He blinks a couple of times, clicks "close," and there . . . he won. So he thinks . . . . I guarantee that if this is your approach to beating porn, or any sin for that matter, you will be a loser. Don't put yourself in the late night one-on-one situation with porn, or I'll add, with your girlfriend either. The win-loss ratio will be laughable. The odds are against you always.

You can't go toe-to-toe with sexual temptation, sin, or Satan. You will get destroyed. Satan hates you. He will hold open the ropes for you to step into the ring so he can obliterate you. Willingly putting yourself before a temptation to prove to yourself and God that you can conquer it is *not* of God. It's of you. It's prideful. It's foolish. In fact, it's unbiblical. And if it's unbiblical, you are already beat. Even your so-called "wins" will have an asterisk by them because they were done outside of how God commands you to deal with sin. Victory will not be sustained.

As men, we're mostly wired to "man up" and fight. But in God's economy, the manly reaction to sexual temptation, sexual sin, and Satan is to run. God surprisingly doesn't coach us to trade punches with sexual temptation, sexual sin, or Satan. He commands us to find His way out and run for our lives. Paul, in 1 Corinthians 6:18 says, "Flee immorality."[9] The New Living translation states it this way, "Run away from sexual sin!" Second Timothy 2:22 says, "Run away from anything that stimulates youthful lust. Follow anything that makes you want to do right."

Rest assured that God promises a way of escape no matter what situation you find yourself in or get yourself into. He provides a way out even when your heart starts to "stray toward her" and "wander down her wayward paths."[10] When you feel an attack coming, or if you're caught in open fire, your first thought should be, *God, get me out of here!* Most likely He's not going to thunder instruction down to you and provide a supernatural way of escape. The escape can be as simple as closing your eyes and/or walking away; texting a brother to tell him of your attack and need for help; calling your mom just to chat; going to the gym and running or lifting weights until you collapse; going somewhere private to get on your face in pleas to God for strength; grabbing the Scriptures, whether by book or online; calling the front desk of the hotel and telling them to shut down cable capabilities to your TV; reading through Proverbs 7; and so forth.

There is always a way out. The problem is, you can ignore it. Or, see how far you can take it and then try to bail at the last minute. I've tried that before. It doesn't work.

Think those thoughts crossed Treadwell's mind? Ignoring danger? Seeing how close he could get without getting attacked? Believing he could escape at the last minute if something happened? It cost him his life.

The Enemy can easily overpower you and entice you with aggressive and available, accessible, and appealing sexual opportunities. Don't test it, or him. Don't be a fool thinking you're in control. You will get eaten alive.

INVENTORY

◆ How has the Enemy made sexual temptation easy and accessible to you?

◆ How has the Enemy aggressively attacked you with sexual temptation?

◆ What ways of escape did God give you in those situations? Did you take them? Why or why not?

◆ What are "escape routes" you can prepare for your life in anticipation of sexual temptation?

BELIEVE NO ONE
WILL KNOW

Come, let's drink our fill in love until morning. Let's enjoy each other's caresses,
for my husband is not home. He's away on a long trip. He has taken a
wallet full of money with him, and he won't return until later in the month.

- PROVERBS 7:18-20

The eye of the adulterer waits for the twilight, Saying
'No eye will see me.' And he disguises his face.

- JOB 24:15

I still dislike taking out the trash. As a kid I hated it. My parents lived on six acres of land. Our family home was about 500 feet off the road. Due to reasons too complicated to explain, we left our garbage by the road of our grandma's driveway. That's the only place the city would pick it up. My grandma lived about 100 or so feet from the road, and about a field-and-a-half away from our house. Even though I was only 14, I was allowed to pile the garbage into the back of Dad's beat-up white pickup truck, drive through the field, and drop off the garbage. I liked doing it about as much as I like punching myself in the mouth.

My dad had just won a 1950 midnight blue, fully restored, Ford pickup truck from a raffle. It was a sharp ride. It still had all of the 1950 trimmings: the big Ford hubcaps, large steering wheel, and so forth. Dad wanted to keep it in pristine condition to sell so he didn't drive it much. He parked it to the side of the driveway to display its glory.

One late weekday afternoon, several months after Dad won the truck, Mom called from work about the garbage in the laundry room. I had procrastinated taking it out for days. She made me stop everything and transport the garbage to grandma's. I seethed. I slung the garbage bags into the back of the old white pickup truck. I jumped in, revved the engine, slammed the gearshift into reverse, and stomped the pedal. Boom! I nailed Dad's new antique truck.

I pulled forward slowly. I nearly puked when I saw the cleft on the front fender. I ran inside and grabbed a hammer. In a panic I tried to beat the caved metal out into its original look. Not even close. My only hope was that Dad would never see it.

Dad's work required him to travel. He left on Mondays and returned on Fridays. It was Friday. I heard him drive up into the driveway. I sat in my room, door closed (and locked), and heart beating out of my chest. He walked by my room toward the closet hamper. Then he walked by again and said hi through my bedroom door.

We ate dinner that night. Not a word was mentioned about the truck. Saturday morning, afternoon, and night, he never said a word. God does answer prayer.

Sunday morning I got ready for church. As I was walking out of the door Dad said, "Jarrod, you stay here." The curtain fell. He knew it all along. I was busted.

THE WAY OF SIN

The seduction of the Proverbs 7 young man has reached the pinnacle. She flat out offers him amazing sex. The bellringer is that she is a married woman. And if there was any reservation on his part of getting caught by her husband, she crushes that concern: "My husband is not home. He's away on a *long* trip."[1] She added that her husband made a withdrawal of a wallet full of money and was gone for nearly a month. This clinched it for him. His testosterone clouded the possibilities that her husband could come home early with roses. She believes her husband will never know. Even worse, he believes it.

When it comes to sexual temptation, we don't have to take it as far as sleeping with another man's wife. Let's talk porn again. How does porn addiction happen? It starts out as a curiosity. The curiosity becomes interest, the interest becomes obsession, and the obsession becomes addiction.[2] That's the way of porn. And secrecy leads the way. The longer the secret wins out, the more you're convinced that no one will find out. It's a pride thing. You're too clever and careful to get caught. But in God's economy, pride comes before destruction.

FALLEN

I've shared the platform with people who have fallen to sexual sin over the years. I think of two at this moment. One fell to a porn addiction gone public and the other to committing adultery on his wife. Both lost their ministries.

One of these men I held in high esteem. As a young man I had been a part of many crowds led by this worship leader. God used this man mightily to lead me into the presence of God. To share the platform with him years later was a gift. I still consider him a dear friend. I love him and pray for him and his family. My heart is still burdened for him. But I cringe and hurt over the blow that the kingdom of God took with his sin. Praise God, His kingdom cannot be stopped.

We haven't talked in a long time. I don't know where he is with the Lord but I do know his marriage is still in tact. I celebrate the truth that through his confession and repentance he will find the grace and forgiveness of Jesus, and hopefully the grace and forgiveness of his wife and kids.

I think back to some downtime I spent with these two friends years ago, before their sin was brought to light. I remember now how I was taken back a bit by certain comments they made in jest about sex. Nothing overt, just out of character. I wish I'd been discerning enough to take it more seriously. I wish I'd been brave enough at the time to call them on it.

For what it's worth I believe these men fell into sexual sin through pride. I think they began taking their gifts and success for granted. They could have been burned out as well but that was never the impression I got (nor is it any kind of excuse). Jesus faded from being the central place of their lives and ministry. Sexual sin either filled the place or was part of the problem. It's possible that through pride they succumbed to a tidbit of sexual temptation. Then it festered. Then it grew. Then it thrived. And the horror of it all is they got away with it, initially. They believed no one would know. But God knew. And He exposed them.

EXPOSED

If you are keeping sexual secrets in your life, you are in trouble. You're falling deeper and deeper into a pit that you will battle to get out of for the rest of your life. Your mind is in peril, your relationships are at risk, your life near ruin. You will be found out. According to Job, the adulterer says, "no eye will see me."[3] Are you suckering yourself into believing that nobody will know of your sexual sin? Are you thinking that you have it all under control, under disguise, so that no one will find out? In fact, you may have sexual sin in your life brilliantly hidden, covered, disguised. But dare to face the inevitable: No secret is kept before God. He knows all thoughts, motives, pursuits, and secrets. It's just a matter of time before God exposes you.

> For the ways of a man are before the eyes of the LORD, And He watches all his paths. [4]

> Don't be mislead. You can't ignore God and get away with it. You will always reap what you sow. [5]

Everything that is now hidden or secret will eventually be brought to light. Anyone who is willing to hear should listen and understand.[6]

Don't ignore God's call to you. Your secret will be brought to light.

Confess your sin to the Lord. Repent before Him. Pray for grace, courage, and strength to handle the fallout. I'll be up front with you. The rubble will come down on and around your family. Plead for them. Confess to your wife, your parents, your church, your pastor, and/or your best friend. It will be painful. Still, expose yourself before you are exposed. Stop trying to convince yourself that you won't be found out. Don't make a bargain with God that if you confess and repent now, He'll let you off the hook. Maybe. But sin you commit in the past, especially sexual sin, tends to haunt you. More devastating and likely is that it will come to light weeks, months, or even years down the road.

Stop hiding. Face the consequences now in the name of Jesus. By the goodness of His grace, trust the Lord with the repercussions of your confession no matter how life-wrenching and relationally impacting it may be. I would encourage you to have a trusted friend, a pastor perhaps, to go through this time with you and support you as you confess your sexual sin to Jesus and your loved ones. Your friend or pastor will help bear the burden with you, pray for you, encourage you. I think of how a fellow soldier throws an arm around the waist of wounded soldier while the wounded soldier throws his arm around the neck of his comrade. And they walk and limp together through the fallout around them. You need that comrade. You need that one who supports you, prays for you, and helps carry you through the debris of consequences.

God is intensely passionate for the sexual purity of your heart and body: "The body is not for sexual immorality but for the Lord, and the Lord for the body."[7] He's so passionate in fact that He will expose you though it costs you your ministry and potentially your marriage and other relationships. He loves you enough to expose you even if it means bringing seemingly detrimental repercussions to His kingdom. In the big picture, He wants all of you, especially your holiness.

Endure [the Lord's discipline]: God is dealing with you as sons. For what son is there with whom a father does not discipline? But if you are without discipline—which we all receive—then you are illegitimate children and not sons. Furthermore, we had natural fathers discipline us, and we respected them. Shouldn't we submit even more to the Father of spirits and live? For they disciplined us for a short time based on what seemed good to them, but He does it for our benefit , so that we can share His holiness. No discpline seems enjoyable at the time, but painful. Later on, however, it yields the fruit of peace and righteousness to those who have been trained by it.[8]

VIBES

God knows your sin. He will expose it. His method of bringing your sin to light might not be through the five o'clock news, though according to the words of singer/songwriter Derek Webb during a concert in Birmingham, Alabama a few years ago, that would be the best thing for you (and all of us, for that matter). That way you're completely exposed to everybody all at once with nowhere to run. Excuses and denial becomes irrelevant. Confession, which means the same as "agree with," would be the only option. Then repentance, hopefully, would follow.

But God is more subtle than that. I believe He will ordain a person to call you out or find you out. This is a merciful move of God into your private sexual sin. You'll be more apt to confess and repent when someone is on to your sin. This prevents you from running from it, or going through the spiritual, mental, and relational gymnastics of rationalizing your sin.

There are Christian family, friends, and colleagues in your life with the gift of discernment. They know you all too well. You may think you've been careful and clever. You haven't. They're picking up vibes. They know you too well. The countdown is on to when they'll officially discover you or they'll confront you. This could be a parent, a pastor, your boss, your wife, or your new buddy from small group Bible study.

I believe you know they already know. For example, when you're around them you feel strangely vulnerable, suspicious, and uncomfortable. You have a vibe that they're on to you but you just don't see how. God's mercy at work in you and around you is how. They know.

Maybe you have already been confronted at some level. Your friend, or dad, or pastor didn't know exactly what you were hiding in your life but they asked you a certain kind of question, or made a type of comment, or simply asked if everything is okay with you. In other words, they don't know your particular sin but they know sin is there. And if they've gone so far to risk a comfortable relationship with you by asking some probing questions about your life, they care. This is your opportunity, God's providential opportunity for you to go to that friend, family, or pastor, and confess your sin as if it were seen on the five o'clock news. Renounce any notion of believing that no one will know about your sin.

NOW OR LATER

The antique truck would never look the same again. But Dad wasn't upset just about the truck. Something else took a dent that day—Dad's trust in me. I lied to him. I tried to deceive him. He was deeply disappointed about my deception. I still remember his words, "Jarrod, you lied! Why did you lie? Never lie to me."

I lived in denial. I audaciously believed that I had beaten the consequences of my action. I didn't consider the cost of what I had done to the truck, nor to Dad's trust in me. I was a fool.

You can't lie to God, but you can lie to yourself. You can convince yourself that whatever sexual sin you are pursuing is hidden. Right now if you are in sexual sin, consider yourself busted. God is speaking through these words to tell you. Confess it to Him. Again, confess means to agree. Agree with Him that you've been living in sin. Repent. Tell Him what He already knows. Quit living the lie. It's better to accept the fallout now than later when someone catches you with your pants down, so to speak. A dented truck is better than a wrecked truck. And an exposed lie of sexual sin is better than a life ruined by sexual sin.

INVENTORY

◆ Do you or have you ever struggled with pornography? How did you get to that place? What will it take to conquer it? Can you ever fully have victory?

◆ What sexual sin are you "disguising" in your life?

◆ If Jesus exposed sexual sin in your life right now, what would everyone discover? How would it affect you and them?

◆ Will you confess sexual sin right now to God, your wife, and/or pastor, or your brothers in Christ? Why or why not?

◆ Have you established accountability in your life? Where are you not accountable?

TAKE JUST
ONE MORE LOOK

He followed her at once, like an ox going to the slaughter
or like a trapped stag, awaiting the arrow that would pierce its heart.
He was like a bird flying into a snare, little knowing
it would cost him his life.

- PROVERBS 7:22-23

The crystal-meth of sexual obsession is Internet sex.[1] Stay with me.

When I was a kid, pornography wasn't readily available. You could get it only through a friend's dad's hidden porn collection or finding magazines under bridges. Today it's as easy to find as Chinese takeout. Online videos, chat rooms, games, photogalleries, and virtual reality provide a plethora of avenues through which you can not only get porn but also actually *experience* it.[2] In other words, you can click online and have virtual sex. You can explore fantasies, flirt nastily, and get "intimate" in cyberspace. And here's the kicker: You can do it *safely* and *anonymously* in the privacy of your own bedroom, office, or hotel room.

Safely and anonymously. These are the lies of pornography. It's safe. It's

not affecting anyone else. It's not physical. It's not hurting you or your reputation. It's not premarital sex or adultery. It's simply the "menu;" you're not
eating from it; you're just looking at it. Sound familiar?

After all, it's anonymous. You can't be recognized. You don't have to use
your real name or personal e-mail address. It's not like walking into a novelty
shop right off the interstate and getting spotted. Right?

GIVE IT TO ME ONE MORE TIME

With Internet sex being available at the tap of the mouse, the temptation to
look just one more time can come easily. It can come particularly easy when
the thumbnail of the online video catches your eye, or that attachment comes
on the e-mail, or the blinking pop-up promising never-before-seen sexual
content appears front-and-center on your computer screen. These moments
bring about the "one more time" rationale. I mean after all, you may have
finally arrived to a place where you're conquering the stuff. It doesn't have
the grip on you it once did. You've done better at avoiding it and fighting
off the temptation recently. Accountability with a buddy has actually made
a huge difference. But there it is right in front of you. Just one more look
won't sink you. Or will it?

FATAL ATTRACTION

Solomon uses stunning metaphors about the deadliness of sexual sin. Like an
ox going to the butcher, a deer snared in the corner with an arrow missiling
toward its heart, like a bird sailing into a trap, all of them clueless that they
will lose their lives. This is the picture for the cost of sexual sin, whether for
those who try it for the first time or look for the thousandth time.

The ox has probably been in the pen behind the butcher's house since it
was a calf. The butcher may have fed it, petted it, spoke sweetly and softly
to it.

The deer probably played around the snare for years. It may have eaten
around it and even paused from time to time to sniff it. Then again, it may

have been caught a couple of times but managed to escape.

The bird might have sat right beside the trap time and time again without noticing it. It could have actually stepped right into the middle of the trap without knowing it, but nothing happened.

Here's the bottom line: they were deceived. Without warning they were trapped and destroyed. This is what you can expect with sexual sin. You can checkout porn for the first time, but after that first look you can become brainwashed into obsession. Or you can view porn for years and think you're safe from its effects. All the while it's the butcher petting you, speaking softly, with his blade raised over your head. Perhaps you almost got caught in your sin a few times, but you felt like you got away with minimal injury. The fact of the matter is that when you least expect it, the blade of sexual obsession and the jaws of sexual addiction can slam down and ruin you. That one last look can cost you.

SEXUAL OPIATES

Crystal-meth. I've never been a user. But I've read about what this drug can do to you. Apparently, when you smoke crystal-meth, opiates, better known as endorphins, are released in your brain that can create powerful pleasure and addiction. In a similar way pornography and masturbation have the same effect as crystal-meth. Powerful endorphins are released through sexual arousal and climax. The brain says, "That feels good. Give me more. Do it again." These endorphins connect your experience of intense pleasure to the images you look at and methods you physically undertake to gain the pleasure. If you're a Christ-follower, conviction and guilt follows because you're encountering sexual pleasure outside of the will of God. Though you feel sorrowful and regretful afterward, you're becoming more and more mastered by the pornography and sexual pleasure. Over time, you find yourself unable to resist the urge to indulge yourself. In other words, you're addicted.

This addiction is powerful. Sexual arousal and release through pornography produces *natural* endorphins in the brain. Crystal-meth produces *chemical* endorphins in the brain. According to the experts, because the "feel-good" endorphins released by the brain through porn are natural, and not chemical duplicates, porn is more addictive than a drug.

> When pornography is combined with sexual release, as in masturbation, and the naturally occurring [endorphins] are set free all over the brain, this is a high reward for the brain. Because it is not a chemical imitation, it's even more addictive.[3]

Again, I personally have never used crystal-meth but I have experienced the difficulties of quitting something addictive. Cigarettes. After college, I smoked about half-a-pack of cigarettes a day for two years. Smoking cigarettes doesn't send you to hell mind you. However, I personally realized they are completely unhealthy and they have a bad stigma. And to top it off, they are *aggressively* addictive.

Cigarettes had such a grip on me. Endorphins, no doubt. I found myself constantly thinking about them. I schemed and planned how to sneak a smoke. I was obsessed and addicted, literally. I daydreamed about smoking during the day. I planned times, places, and driving routes, so I could experience my pleasure. I avoided friends and family because I didn't want them to smell cigarette smoke on me. When I was around them, I would make excuses to go run an errand so that I could smoke.

I would stand behind a grocery store walls with my shirt off, holding the cigarette out from me at about arm's length while I smoked so I could keep the smell off me. Yes, a bit extreme. When I visited friends and family, I looked for the first opportunity to leave so I could go smoke. I valued the cigarette more than my relationships. That is no overstatement. If I was hindered from sneaking a smoke by friends or family I'd get agitated. Do you see where this is going?

PORN ADDICT

If an unprofitable addiction to tobacco could get so out of control as to affect my pocketbook, my conscience, my health, my relationships, my sanity, can you imagine the sin of porn addiction? Are you a porn addict? Ask yourself these questions:

- Do you use pornography to escape from life?
- Do you willingly risk your job and relationships in order to view pornography?
- Do you constantly battle with controlling your thoughts and preventing thoughts about how and when you can view pornography?
- Do you look through books, flip through TV channels, surf through newspaper ads, or thumb through magazines, to find something sexual?
- Have you ever trashed your porn stash, put blocks on your computer, and committed never to look at porn again, only to take just one more look, then another, and another?

In summary, if you find yourself constantly thinking about sex and porn, daydreaming about another hit, planning times and places, avoiding relationships, sneaking around for moments of pleasure, and going to bizarre extremes to maintain your secrecy, there is no question that you are obsessed and addicted.

POWERLESS GUILT

Guilt will not free you from your addiction. Guilt can actually drive you deeper into it. In other words, the tables are turned to where the very addiction you feel guilty about is what you use to medicate the guilt. Sexual sin brings guilt. Guilt brings self-pity. Self-pity needs medicating. The addiction medicates the guilt and self-pity. This vicious cycle can take you through a thousand "just one more look(s)."

Sexual obsession and addiction can sear your conscience deeply; scar your emotional, spiritual, and mental health profoundly; damage your relationships severely, and ruin your life ultimately.

QUITTING ADDICTIONS

Let me tell you how I quit smoking. Watch for the comparisons to beating sexual sin. This list is not exhaustive by any means but it's a start.

One, I began to associate cigarettes with everything negative in my life—the sneaking around, the smell, the taste, the chains. I got sick of it. I was fed up with the labor of secrecy especially. If my secret got exposed, as with any other "secret" in one's life getting exposed, it might draw further questions from people about what else I might be hiding in my life.

Simply what positive anything is porn bringing to your life? Lust will never, ever, satisfy. You can't get enough. Notice I said that I smoked half-a-pack of cigarettes a day (and climbing), not a half-a-cigarette a day. I could never get enough. You can never get enough sexual anything to gratify you totally. You will always want more.

Two, I knew the disappointment it would bring to my family. I knew the confusion it might bring to people who looked up to me. The negative stigma of smoking can be jolting. I deeply care about what my friends and family think of me. It would have been embarrassing and saddening for me to see their disappointment and confusion.

Sexual sin secrets coming to light will bring disappointment and disillusionment to family, friends, and those who admire you. In addition, I think there is a huge difference in getting exposed unwillingly than in willingly exposing yourself. Willingly exposing yourself says so much about your heart and desire for a pure character. It reveals that you recognize your sin and helplessness. You're sick of the deception so your confessing and repenting the best and only way you know how. You are seeking help and mercy from those you love and who love you. Those who love you would recognize this. Otherwise, if your secret is *discovered* then you simply got caught.

Three, I began to see the folly of smoking. I didn't want lung cancer. Sucking in toxic fumes just didn't seem normal or right for me.

Consider just for a moment how *not* normal pornography is. It is not reality. It's an act with actors and actresses directed for sexual performances. It's not like these encounters happen in people's lives as a pattern. It's bogus not to think that in the real world there can be a heavy price to pay for even a hint of this kind of sexual encounter. Not to mention the stuff is edited and airbrushed. And the effects on the lives and minds of the "actors" aren't part of the picture either. STDs, AIDS, and constant tests for STDs and AIDS as a way of life? Not normal.

Finally, I quit smoking because God broke my heart. They were my master, and Jesus wasn't. And I wanted Jesus to break my heart. I begged Him to give me a hatred for anything that obsessed me more than Him.

Will you pray the same for your obsession with porn and other sexual sin? Will you pray He break your heart in that sexual sin will no longer be your master, and that only Jesus be your Master? I begged Jesus for help and deliverance and victory over cigarettes. Beg the same about your sexual sin. In moments of weakness I am tempted to be numb and self-medicate myself with nicotine. But I know it will not make my issues go away. And cost-free smoking is not reality. Same for sexual sin. It's alluring, but it will not make your issues go away. The fake glamour and cost-free pleasure is not reality.

A POTENT WORD

Not only can God break your heart over your sexual sin, but also He can empower you to conquer it. God's Word, i.e., Proverbs 7, is powerful in my personal life. "For the word of God is living and effective and sharper than any two-edged sword, penetrating as far as to divide soul and spirit joints and marrow; it is a judge of the ideas and thoughts of the heart."[4] God declared through the prophet Jeremiah that His Word is "like a fire and a hammer that shatters the rock."[5] God's Word is potent. Is it any wonder then that God, through Solomon, began Proverbs 7 saying, "My son, keep my *words* . . ."?[6]

I seek to meditate on the Scriptures so that my mind won't dwell on sexual temptations and sin. I'm not perfect at the meditating, mind you, but I try. I try because I need Scripture to guard me and empower me. I'm just not strong enough without it. By default I lean toward ruin. It's a sin thing. But I believe that God's Word is a sword that slits the throat of sexual sin.

PRAYER ALERT

Specific prayer in the area alone—prayer for purity, integrity, strength, and alertness to the schemes of the Devil—I can't do without. The apostle Paul said, "Devote yourselves to prayer with an *alert* mind . . . ."[7] Prayer keeps me alert to the temptations. Specific prayer about sexual temptation prepares my mind and spirit. It reminds me that temptations are coming at me that day. Then when the temptations come, I reflect on my prayer, act on my prayer, and enter back into prayer about the temptation before me. In prayer I find strength and victory. Prayer is a shield against ruin.

ACCOUNTABILITY

We all need accountability in our lives. King Solomon states, "As iron sharpens iron, a friend sharpens a friend."[8] Also, he says, "Wounds from a friend are better than kisses from an enemy."[9] But at the end of the day, accountability can affect only our actions. And that is not as important as a real "heart change." The heart is the ultimate issue. King Solomon would agree. He states, "*Above all else,* guard your heart, for it affects everything you do."[10] Guarding your heart at all times, confession and repentance before Christ, and the Spirit of Christ in you, is what brings about true and sustained heart change, not accountability.

However, accountability can be used of God to foster heart change. The fact that you would seek accountability speaks much about your desire for heart and life change. If you suffer from sexual addiction, you need a friend or mentor to ask you tough sexual questions on a consistent basis. Personally, in terms of accountability for my life, it helps that sexual issues are not the only topic of discussion. It's more a friendship in which we spur each other on to loving and following Jesus in all areas. In my opinion, accountability should be less structured and "businesslike," and more organic, vulnerable, and authentic. It should be natural to a friendship. Meeting on a forced topic of conversation which may have begun on a committed note can quickly become dreadful, even when there's no sexual sin. If you find a good friend that you trust to provide you with accountability, it needs to be relationship-driven rather than agenda-driven.

When my friend and I meet, sexual accountability is not the goal of our time together. It's not an "accountability" time of month. We're just hanging out. But when he asks me about sexual temptation in my life, I take a strong inventory. It's not a routine question. It's not what we hang out for. It's not for an agenda. I know that we are spending time together because there is a genuine relationship and a genuine concern for my life. So if he mentions sexual purity, I know there is a reason God laid it on his heart to ask me at that specific time and place. The timing of his question makes me examine myself closely. I know that God uses that moment to keep me from potentially ruining my life.

In the same vein, remember that this style of accountability may not be what you need right now. You may need the "in your face" accountability, especially if you found yourself answering "yes" to a lot of the questions in the addiction section on the previous pages. The first steps in breaking a serious addiction are becoming humble, vulnerable, and honestly answering the tough questions. Ask your accountability partner to get "in your face" on a regular basis. Find folks to hold you accountable who you know will get into your business and won't let you off easy.

FINDING ACCOUNTABILITY

Don't have anyone in your life? Don't know where to start? First, you may need professional help. You need to see a licensed, professional, Christian counselor. Many churches and Christian organizations provide counselors who are free or charge a minimum fee. Perhaps whatever you've been spending on your addiction can be transferred to spending on counseling. Giving up your daily latte would be worth using that money to get professional help for your addiction. And realize that this isn't a quick fix. Before your addiction can be dealt with, there may be deeper issues in your life that need to be brought to the surface.

If you find that porn is more of a struggle than an addiction (but this applies to addicts also), you need to proactively pursue another godly man and friend for aggressive accountability. Pray for who that certain godly man might be in your life. Then pray for courage to approach him, confess to him, and ask him for help.

Ask if you could meet with him personally once a week, or every two weeks, or once a month, depending on his availability. At the least ask if he would e-mail or call you periodically during the week to ask you the tough questions about where your eyes, ears, hands, and mind have been. There is software available now that can keep him posted on what sites you've been visiting on the net too.[11] The goal is for Christ to use him to move you toward repentance and purity. This entails you giving him permission to be confrontational with you when needed. Accountability is not for the faint of heart.

WHERE TO LOOK

When the "one more look" drags you toward sexual sin, take ten long looks at the cross of Jesus.[12] Think about Jesus' stunning sacrifice, His great love, His awesome freedom, and His gripping grace gifted to you when He saved you by His death on the cross. You are free from addiction and free from struggle and free from sin because He beat it all on the cross. You are no longer a slave to your lusts. You are a son of His love and glory. So embrace the truth and live it by constant repentance and faith. Prayer and His Word empower you to live in repentance and faith. If you are a Christian, God's Spirit indwells you and you dwell within Him; the power given Christ to conquer death is granted to you to conquer sexual sin.[13] You can conquer sexual addiction by confessing and repenting to Christ, keeping your eyes on Christ, and meditating on who you are in Christ.

> For we died and were buried with Christ by baptism. And just as Christ was raised from the dead by the glorious power of the Father, now we also may live new lives.

Since we have been united with Him in His death, we will also be raised as he was. Our old sinful selves were crucifed with Christ so that sin might lose its power in our lives. We are no longer slaves to sin. For when we died with Christ we were set free from the power of sin. And since we died with Christ we know we will also share his new life. We are sure of this because Christ rose from the dead, and he will never die again. Death no longer has any power over him. He died once to defeat sin, and now he lives for the glory of God. So you should consider yourselves dead to sin and able to live for the glory of God through Christ Jesus.

Do not let sin control the way you live; do not give in to its lustful desires. Do not let any part of your body become a tool of wickedness, to be used for sinning. Instead, give yourselves completely to God since you have been given a new life. And use your whole body as a tool to do what is right for the glory of God. Sin is no longer your master, for you are no longer subject to the law which enslaves you to sin. Instead, you are free by God's grace.[14]

Looking at Jesus keeps you blind to ruin.

INVENTORY

◆ What does it mean to you that Solomon compared committing sexual sin to an ox going to the butcher, a deer getting shot with an arrow, and a bird caught in a trap?

◆ Do you agree that porn is not reality? Why? How can this help you in temptation?

◆ Have you ever found yourself sneaking around, daydreaming about, and planning how you can get a hit of porn? Why are you doing it?

◆ What steps will you take to get accountability into your life?

◆ How can Romans 6 empower you to break the chains of addiction and struggle with porn?

◆ Pray that God will give you a passionate hatred for pornography and any form of sexual sin.

◆ I'd encourage you to fast, pray, indeed plead, that God break your heart and the chains of your sexual sin.

TIP #6

ACT WITHOUT THINKING

Suddenly he follows…

—Proverbs 7:22

One of my best friends was car shopping a few years ago. He walked into a dealership and was seduced by a dark green, loaded-to-the-nines, Cadillac Escalade. He was hooked. He bought it within minutes.

I don't know much about buying cars. I especially don't know a thing about buying the likes of a Cadillac Escalade. I've bought only one car my whole life—a 1995 Mazda 626, and my dad did the wheeling and dealing. I've been told that the worst mistake you can make when buying a car is doing so suddenly and impulsively. My dad is big on not buying anything impulsively. Before he buys anything he will take days, sometimes weeks, to mull it over. He will consider the cost, do research on the brand, and turn the positive and negative possibilities of ownership over and over again in his mind. When he comes to a decision, he stands firm on it. I've seen him walk away from various major purchases because upon reflection he didn't have a good vibe about it. Somewhere in life Dad learned the hard way—you don't buy impulsively. He's never forgotten it. Now he gives careful thought to what comes with a price tag. I, on the other hand, am still learning.

My buddy is still learning too. He didn't give his purchase any thought at all. He was gripped by the Escalade's style, its feel, its beauty. He test drove it and was hooked. He couldn't help himself. He bought it without thinking.

However, in the days following, he couldn't sleep. He'd spent a fortune on this vehicle. It was out of his budget-zone and he realized it after the fact. Reality over what he'd done set in. He took the vehicle back to the dealership three or four days later. He begged them to take it back. The dealership refused him without batting an eyelash. He alone was the one to blame for his decision. He acted without thinking. And he paid through the nose for it.

In Proverbs 7, Solomon is observing the young man. He doesn't just say, "He follows her." Rather, "He *suddenly* follows her."[1] Suddenly implies impulsive. Impulsive actions are perilous. On a grand scale they can ruin. On a lesser than grand scale, they can bring intense regret. This goes for any category of life.

FREE PASSES

The young man's downfall was that he didn't head his temptation off at the pass. When his lust awakened, he should have closed his eyes, turned his head, and walked the other way, not near the door of her house. When she approached him, he should have run for his life.

Stop where you are. Think about what you are doing. Like the young man of Proverbs 7, are you looking at the sticker price of what wrong choices will cost you? Are you buying in to sexual sin out of emotion and testosterone? If you're married, you know if you are in a questionable "friendship" with a woman right now. Don't deny your pull toward to her. Give your actions and relationships some very, very deep thought. As the cliché goes, "Call a spade a spade." End the "friendship." In terms of porn, give the password of your computer to your wife and encourage her to check your e-mails for you. Give your friends free reign to your computer. In other words, if your buddy needs to check his e-mail on your computer, or surf the 'net, you shouldn't have to fear what could he could find there.

If you're single, you are in a tough spot. I've been there; I was single for 31 years. You are not exempt from those dangerous "friendships" either. Guard your life, and hers. You are also in the unfortunate position that it is easier to keep porn hidden in your life. Make yourself an aquarium to brothers in Christ. Allow anyone and everyone to have a free pass to your computer and your bedroom drawers. Give free access to your mom. Mom-regulated accountability is some of the most dependable accountability on the planet

CHEAP AND EASY

Christie and I were given a week's timeshare in Newport, Rhode Island for our honeymoon. Christie wanted to do something fun that included the ocean. I, being the big spender, decided we would rent a dinghy and cruise the bay. I didn't know what a dinghy was. But it cost only $50 for an hour.

A dinghy is basically a big rubber bathtub with a weed-eater on the back. When we arrived at the pier I met the owner at his rental booth. We made our way to the dinghy. Christie crawled in. I sort of slid and tumbled in. The motor was a small outboard. The steering was in the form of a stick-like handle grip that protruded from the motor into my back. I sat facing the front. I had to reach behind me to steer the boat by the handle. There was also a little lever on the engine itself I had to work separately to accelerate and decelerate the dinghy. The owner asked, "Have you ever driven one of these?" "Sure," I answered. Not totally trusting my answer, he launched into his bit on how to operate it. All I was thinking was "yada-yada, whatever. How hard can it be to drive a '*dinghy*?"

The little engine wheezed to life. I smiled at Christie and said, "Welcome to the love boat, baby." She was not impressed. Then I revved the engine. It launched out of its little harbor. I had a death grip on the steering stick. The boat was swinging violently left and right. The little dinghy was out of control. I couldn't figure out that you had to push the steering stick right to make the boat go left, and then left to make the boat go right. I panicked. We hadn't made it five feet from the rental booth and we were doing donuts. I screamed like a seven-year-old girl.

The dinghy took on a life of its own. It set its sights for an adjacent pier. We braced ourselves. "Bam," then "bam, bam, bam." The dinghy would bounce off the pier only to shake it off, gather steam, and plunge ahead into the pier again. Christie yelled, "Jarrod, you're hitting the pier!" I shouted back, "You think?!" I reached behind me and started pushing and jerking on anything that protruded from the engine. The engine finally shut down.

It would have behooved me to give some thought to what I was getting myself, and Christie, into. I should have listened and asked more questions. What looked innocent enough on the outside proved to be a monster. It was cheap and looked easy. It was attractive because it was cheap and easy. But I learned again that opportunities and looks are deceptive. And many times anything that is cheap, easy, and just attractive on the outside, you usually pay more for in the end.

FIXED

Porn is attractive. It's cheap. It's easy. It involves no commitment. It doesn't involve the hard work of intimacy. It doesn't involve the labor of communicating, dealing with issues, and bearing the burdens of relationship. It's a fix. It's an appeal to a carnal, animal, side of us. It's worth mentioning that sex and the desires thereof are a gift of God. Sin has fractured our God-given desires though. Pure, God-given desire for sexual intimacy in marriage has been infected with animalistic lust. Porn engages that lust. Women then, particularly those who are "forbidden fruit," become objects to satisfy that animal appetite.

When you act without thinking, you place yourself in a situation where you can't stop. It can happen with porn. Or it can begin with friendship with a woman that gets a little too vulnerable, then emotional, and finally physical. You didn't think through where that "friendship" could take you. You ignored or denied the attraction that stirred in you.

Also, you can act without thinking when she looks at you, grins at you, tilts her head back and giggles at everything you say. You can get caught up in the net of an attractive, needy, "easy" woman. Before you can say "ruin," your lust is tapped. Your eyes glaze over, and so does your willpower. God's grace of escape is at your fingertips but you're numbed and deafened by your lust. The descent has begun. Momentum is gained toward ruin. But strangely, it feels good. You just can't help yourself.

The young man Solomon is watching has acted on his lust. The woman in the last 21 verses has set him up. He should have walked away at verse six. But there were no boundaries in his life. The opportunity was just too easy, unshakably enticing. Adventure awaited him. According to the immoral woman, it was risk free. Her husband was out of town. She's attractive, she's cheap, and she's easy. Or she's attractive because she's cheap and easy.

ACCOUNTABILITY CO-DEPENDENCE

As you've seen in the previous chapter I'm a fan of accountability but with reservations. King Solomon expresses the wisdom of accountability but at the same time says *"above all else* guard your heart."[2] In light of accountability he points to it being relationally-driven not agenda-driven. He speaks of *friends* sharpening *friends,* and the "wounds of a *friend . . .".*[3]

You read in the last chapter that I have this kind of friendship accountability in my own life. On the other hand, I also stated that some men might be in a place where they need official (agenda-driven) accountability in their life due to the depth of their struggle. Either way, we all need it. Still you can't base obedience to Jesus on accountability. True obedience flows from the heart not accountability. With that said, I'll go further now to say that accountability can actually hinder authentic heart change because of co-dependence upon it. Indeed, I feel that accountability can become overrated and even dangerous to some degree by preventing true heart change.

For example, you can meet for coffee once a week with a godly friend for the tough questions, and that's a good thing. And you can set up software on your computer that e-mails your friend when you go to a Web site that you should not go to, also a good system. But even if you are changing habits and the accountability appears to be working from the outside, the bigger issue is still your heart. Jesus says that all the evil resides in your heart: "For from the heart come evil thoughts . . . adultery, all other sexual immorality."[4]

If your accountability time consistently revolves around the words, "I'm still struggling," there needs to be a thorough heart check. Likewise if all you've done is become more religious or moral in not committing sexual sin, you've missed it there too.

Therefore if change is happening only on the outside but your heart is still burning with lust, what to do? Get on your knees and beg Jesus to do a heart cleanse on you. King David pleaded with God to, "Create in me a clean heart, O God. Renew a right spirit within me."[5] I bet he cried that on his knees, alone. Accountability must carry the prayerful pursuit of a clean heart as the laser-light focus.

SET THE BEAD

Deal with your heart by submitting your mind. Wake up in the morning and as you step out of your bed, pray, "Lord, I give you my mind today. I worship you with my mind. I surrender my mind to you all day and in every way." Desire the mind of Christ. Plead with Him to give you a pure mind and then put action behind it. Paul states, "Fix your thoughts on what is true and honorable and right. Think about things that are pure and lovely and admirable. Think about things that are excellent and worthy of praise."[6] "Fix" is an action word. It's discipline to adjust and readjust your mind to the things of God.

You will not stumble onto purity. You will not trip over godliness and holiness of mind and heart. You have to aim for it. Listen to Job's aim: "I made a covenant with my eyes not to lust upon a young woman."[7] You have to set the bead of your eyes, heart, and mind upon the Scriptures, purity, and godliness.

PAYING THROUGH THE NOSE

Take heed. Though sexual opportunity can be attractive, easy, and cheap, it will cost you more down the line. I have a dinghy experience to prove it. One thoughtless choice can slam you into a pier of ruin.

Indeed a sudden choice might cost you more than you bargained for. Just ask my buddy with the Cadillac Escalade. As soon as he drove it off the lot, it depreciated drastically. He could sell it but he'd lose his financial rear end. Due to his impulsive decision, he had to live with the loss. In terms of sexual temptation, one thoughtless, sudden, impulsive choice can make you pay through the nose for the rest of your life. In other words, it can ruin you.

INVENTORY

◆ Are you giving *careful* thought to the price you would pay for a sexual sin in your life? Explain.

◆ Read Ephesians 6:11. Are you alert and prepared for the Devil's schemes through sexual temptation so that you will not make an impulsive choice toward ruin?

◆ Are you in the pattern of "Pray for me; *I'm still struggling*"? What actions must you take to break the pattern?

◆ How will you set the bead of your heart and mind on purity?

◆ For further reflection, flip to the appendix in the back of the book to read the article by Randy Alcorn, titled, "Deterring Immorality by Counting Its Cost: An Exorbitant Price of Sexual Sin."

TIP
#7

THINK YOU'RE
THE EXCEPTION

For she has been the ruin of many;
numerous men have been her victims.
Her house is the road to the grave.
Her bedroom is the den of death.

- PROVERBS 7:26-27

On Januray 26, 1972, Vesna Vulovic, a flight attendant from the Former Republic of Yugoslavia (now the Federation of Serbia and Montenegro), was aboard a DC-9 flight that blew up over Czechslovakia (now the Czech Republic). A terrorist bomb was thought to be the cause. All passengers died except Vesna. She survived a 33,300-foot free fall from the sky. Let me repeat. Vesna lived following a super high, one-minute-plus plunge out of the sky. A nurse saw Vesna's legs sticking out of the plane's fuselage. Vesna had two broken legs, was temporarily paralyzed from the waist down, and in a coma. She awoke from her coma three days later.[1]

RARE EXCEPTIONS

Is it just me, or do you think Vesna is the exception to that situation? This is not the norm. You don't see Fox News breaking a story like this . . . ever. Rare is there a survivor of such an ordeal, to say the least.

Similarly, rare is he who escapes spiritual, emotional, physical, relational, fallout over sexual sin. Enter the young man in Proverbs 7 again. His heart was swayed and now he's strayed. Solomon knows what's coming. He's seen it time and again. He's seen so many men fall because they were hardened to truth, not counting the cost, going for experience, acting without thinking, thinking they might be the exception. He's witnessed so much sexual ruin. Solomon pronounces, "For she has been the *ruin* of *many*; *numerous* men have been her victims."[2] Notice the words again: "many" and "numerous." In other words, rare is the one who escapes. Rare are the exceptions. The young man will pay dearly. It's just a matter of time.

PAYDAY

If you think you're clever and careful enough to keep your secrets buried, your payday is coming. And you could pay dearly. You may be retracing your steps, covering your telephone calls, double-deleting your e-mails, viewing porn on a computer other than your own, and so forth. But sooner or later you'll get lazy, comfortable, braver, and sloppy in your secrecy, and the curtain will fall. At the end of the day, when God sets about to get you, you're done. "Don't be misled. Remember that you can't ignore God and get away with it. You will always reap what you sow. Those who live only to satisfy their own sinful desires will harvest the consequences of decay and death."[3]

Just this year a famous itinerant minister who once was a local pastor at a thriving church in my hometown was exposed for adultery. He had maintained an adulterous affair for nearly 20 years. Twenty years. But his day of reckoning came. You have to wonder how long it took for him to be convinced he was the exception to ruin. A month? A year? Nineteen years? The fact that his ministry thrived and grew while he was committing adultery probably heightened his thoughts that he might be the exception. But God set about exposing him, and he was called to the carpet. The fallout of his sexual sin upon his ministry, his former church, his family, and the community was devastating.

Furthermore, can you imagine the fallout on the woman with whom he was having the affair? We often don't consider the trauma she will endure. Imagine the shame, regret, embarrassment, and pain she will experience before her friends and family. As Christian men, we must keep in our minds and hearts that all women are created in the image of God and are loved by Him. Our desire should be to honor all women. Our conviction should be to protect them, even from ourselves.

PALLBEARER

Solomon says that sexual sin is "the road to the grave."[4] Not *a* road to *a* grave, but *the* road to *the* grave. It's a journey that will bury you. It's as if sexual sin is a pallbearer carrying you to the grave of ruin. In physical life, there are no exceptions to the grave. Solomon might have been reflecting on this inevitability in relation to sexual sin. Those in sexual sin who escape the grave of ruin are few. The exceptions are a fraction of the minority. The number of the exceptions is found only to the right of the decimal point.

Sexual sin has snuffed out the life of many marriages. Few have been the exceptions. Sexual sin can put your marriage in the grave. Still, God can resurrect it through confession, repentance, and His forgiveness and grace. God can revive your marriage through your spouse's grace and forgiveness, and through your repentance and renewed vow to her. But that devastation will be tough to forget. Scars will remain. Hopefully God's grace will empower your spouse to grant grace. But do you really want to make the choices to put yourself and your spouse in this potential nightmare?

For those in church leadership, sexual sin can execute your ministry. You won't be the exception here. However, God can still redeem it to the degree that He wills. He can still use you. Yet you will be disqualified from certain avenues of ministry for the rest of your life. The apostle Paul declared, "I discipline my body like an athlete, training it to do what it should. Otherwise, I fear that after preaching to others I myself might be disqualified."[5]

Is sexual sin worth this?

SINFUL SEASONS

Solomon further notes that "her house" (sexual sin) is the way of "descending to the chambers of death."[6] Sexual sin is a downward spiral of your heart, mind, and life into death row. Few are the exception to getting out of death row. This is King Solomon's way of expressing the horror of sexual sin—death. In other words, the cost of sexual sin is of epic proportions. The cost is related to "death." Your heart can become overcome by lust that controls you. Your mind can become consumed with addiction to sexual images (and the actions that follow for sexual release) and darkened to what is normal sexually according to God's will. Ultimately speaking, your life can become ruined by sexual sin—death.

Unrepentant sexual sin could reveal that you are under the sentence of spiritual death. Does sexual sin bring about the eternal death of your soul? Not if you are a Christian. You are saved by grace through faith not by works.[7]

But here's the kicker: True Christians repent. How do you know it is a "season" of sin instead of a life of unbelief in the salvation and lordship of Jesus? You can make a season of sin an excuse for your sin. But the apostle Paul says, "[S]hould we keep on sinning so that God can show us more and more kindness and forgiveness? Of course not! Since we have died to sin, how can we continue to live in it?"[8]

Here's the real problem with saying that you're "still in a season" and telling yourself that it will "end soon, but I'm not ready yet"—you don't love God as much as you love yourself. Period. If at any point in the last two weeks you've actually had the thought process of, "It's just a season; I can stop; God will forgive me," then you owe it to yourself and Jesus to admit, "I don't love God as much as I love myself." Let's be honest here. You know what God thinks. You know what you think. Your actions express what you really believe.

I wonder if you know the direction of this path. Soon you won't ask for God's forgiveness because you'll eventually care less and less that you're sinning against Him. Your heart will grow harder. You'll simply love your sin more than Him. Your season of sin will become your lifestyle of sin. All arrows then point in the direction that you no longer obey Him because you were never truly of Him.[9] To think you won't fall into that possibility is naïve. You're not the exception. Neither am I.

Get right with God. He will forgive you through authentic confession, repentance, and godly sorrow. But the key to it is sorrow and repentance over your sexual sin and not basting in a season of it. "For God can use sorrow in our lives to help us turn away from sin and seek salvation. We will never regret that kind of sorrow. But sorrow without repentance is the kind that results in death."[10]

Keep in mind, however, that you can be sorrowful and guilt-ridden in a season of sexual sin. But are you repenting? You can rationalize your season of sin and be sorrowful over it for a week or eighty years. But will you repent?

CATCH-22

Would you buy into the possibility that a gift from God is to get blindsided by Him and hurled off the road of sexual sin? It's a gift not to be the exception, no matter how much you hope you'll be. If you are a follower of Christ, I believe God will intentionally expose you. It's just a matter of His timing. That exposure though is grace. And if you are a child of God, you will never be the exception to His grace.

Yet a very troubling reality is that you could be the rare exception of *not* getting exposed. You may never get caught by another person. Vesna beat insurmountable odds and lived through her ordeal. You may beat the odds and your sexual sin never be exposed. Or, you could get exposed and ultimately not care or repent. The wrath of God could be upon you, evidenced by the fact that you have not been caught and forced to repent.

We tend to think of God's wrath as fire, brimstone, destruction, and rage. This is true. However, according to Romans 1, God's passive wrath is seen in letting someone get away with his sin. "But God shows His anger from heaven against all sinful, wicked people who push the truth away from themselves."[11] "So God let them go ahead and do whatever shameful things their hearts desired." [12] ". . . God abandoned them to their shameful desires."[13] "[H]e abandoned them to their evil minds and let them do things that should never be done."[14] There are no exceptions for all are under the wrath God other than those who have embraced Jesus as their Savior and Lord. Then that salvation plays itself out publicly through the heart-driven desire to honor Jesus through confession, repentance, and godly living.

SAVING FACE

Sexual sin, particularly pornography, grants a powerful combination: powerful pleasure and easy secrecy. For Christian men to maintain their appearance of being a "great Christian guy," or "godly man," sexual sin is an intoxicating temptation and the ideal sin to nurse in one's life. These men can wholly forget that their sin is against God. Their whole ambition instead is to maintain their Christian witness with no thought toward repentance. In other words, they are wrapped up with protecting their reputation while failing to recognize that the monumental issue is not their embarrassment and shame. The monumental issue is that their sexual sin is an abomination to God. Are *you* one of these men?

PARDONED

I'm persuaded the best thing that can happen is that you *not* be the exception to exposure. It's God's way of showing you mercy. It could save you from very serious implications on your spiritual, emotional, and relational life in the future. I've heard testimonies of married men, even ministers, who after being exposed for their sexual sins, were relieved to be caught. I've seen men collapse back into their chairs, weep in godly sorrow, and look up to God with gratitude and relief. Freedom, though painful, had come. Sexual sin had them imprisoned in the darkness of secrecy and guilt, but God intervened and blasted His light into their prison. The discovery brought embarrassment and trauma to all involved, but the chamber door was ripped off the hinges and the steps ascending to freedom lay before them. Yes, relational consequences awaited, but they were out of death row.

These men were thankful they weren't the exception. They were finally "free." Still, in many cases that freedom came with remarkable pain. That's the trade-off. Very few are the exceptions. But I believe the pain could be more unbearable down the road.

PAINFUL GRACE

Rare is the one who escapes consequences of sexual sin. Many and numerous are the slain, the ruined. Possibilities are that you will not be the exception. Come clean. God is going to expose you anyway. It's just a matter of when He decides the time is right.

Vesna survived the 33,300-foot fall but she still suffered broken bones and was partially paralyzed. But she lived. Brokenness and shock comes with the exposed sin, but so can survival. It will take time for the brokenness to heal. The paralyzed parts of your relationships may slowly gain feeling, but some parts may not . . . I'm just being real. But I do know that Christ Jesus is the forgiver, the lover, the healer, the Savior. He's the Savior of souls, and the Savior of relationships too. He grants grace and can empower others to give it.

POINTS TO PONDER

You wouldn't be foolish enough to think that surviving the impact of a plunge from the sky is the norm, instead of the exception. It's inconceivable. So can we think of sexual sin the same way? When things go wrong in your life and sexual sin looks like an escape, don't even give it consideration.

- Declare sexual sin inconceivable in your life experience.
- Dismiss any thought that you'd be the exception of not being exposed.

- Reflect on the feelings, the repercussions, and the impact your fall would have on your life, on those who love you, and on the ones you love.
- If you get exposed, be thankful. It's a sign of God's grace.

TRADING PLACES

If your sexual sin is exposed I would bet that you and any one of your loved ones would trade places with Vesna. In other words, you would welcome the horror, impact, consequences, and pain of her terrifying fall over what your sexual sin has brought upon you and them. I bet you would trade with Vesna in a heartbeat over your terrifying fall into ruin. Don't be foolish. Don't ever think for a minute that you'll be an exception. You will ruin your life.

INVENTORY

◆ What could be the fall out of sexual sin on those you love and those who love you?

◆ How do you feel about the reality that God would allow someone to keep "getting away" with their sexual sin?

◆ Has God allowed you to get away with your sexual sin? What could this mean for you according to Romans 1? What must you do now in response?

◆ Are you willing *to be made willing* by God to expose yourself? Confess and repent before Christ. Then go confess and repent to your family and friends.

◆ But if you are addicted to sexual sin and too afraid to expose yourself, would you dare pray that God would intervene and expose you? Pray that prayer now.

TIP #8

LEARN BY EXPERIENCE

Always treasure my commands. Obey them and Live!"

– PROVERBS 7:1 2

My mom is a stellar cook. Some of my favorite meals my mom makes are cornbread, black-eyed peas, slaw, and any kind of broiled or fried meat she puts on the table. Growing up, she worked her magic on the electric oven.

I once had a thing about the oven's burners. I would walk into the kitchen after she had turned on the oven and touch each burner as fast as I could. I wanted to see if I was fast enough to keep from getting my hand fried. Mom would say, "Alright, Jarrod, you'd better watch it. You're going to get burned." Seems a no-brainer, I know. But I was 13 years old. Need I say more?

One day I walked into the kitchen and one of the four oven burners had gone from black to orange. Think lava hot. I eyeballed it. Mom said, "Jarrod, I'm telling you . . . you'd better not." I couldn't resist. So with my fingertips I went from burner to burner lightning fast, or so I thought. Then my hand touched the orange eye. Time froze; all feeling departed; my mouth opened but not a sound came out. Then as waves of traumatic pain shot through my hand, time flashed forward to catch up with the moment. From my mouth came the release of primitive screams. I ran around the inside and outside of the house holding my hand like a baby chick. Mom shouted, "I told you, Jarrod! You should have listened to me!"

Profound words, "You should have listened." She gave the facts: The oven burner is hot and you will get burned. But I went the way of experience. The consequence of ignoring the facts and choosing the experience brought me a great deal of pain.

SEXUAL BURNS

Notice Solomon's take on what will bring a great deal of pain, scars, and ultimately ruin into your life.

Entering *[the immoral woman's]* house leads to death; it is the road to hell. The man who visits *her* is doomed. He will never reach the paths of life.[1]

The lips of the immoral woman are as sweet as honey, and her mouth is smoother than oil. But the result is as bitter as poison, sharp as a double-edged sword. *Her* feet go down to death; *her* steps lead straight to the grave. For she does not care about the path to life.[2]

For *a prostitute* will bring you to poverty, and *sleeping with another man's wife* may cost you your very life. Can a man scoop *fire* into his lap and not be burned? Can he walk on hot coals and not burn his feet? So it is with the man who sleeps with another man's wife. He who embraces *her* will not go unpunished.[3]

Solomon seems to drill home the dangers of sexual ruin more than anything else in Proverbs. Chapters five, six, and seven are almost entirely devoted to it. Think carefully about these Scriptures. They can be summed up this way: Sexual immorality (premarital sex, homosexuality, adultery, pornography):

- Leads to death
- Is a road to hell
- Dooms you
- Poisons your soul
- Is a sword that will cut you down
- Leads you to the grave, spiritual and perhaps physical
- Ruins your life
- May cost you your life
- Burns you
- Punishes you

Solomon didn't state these facts for shock value. They are realities. According to the Word of God, if you choose to ignore the facts and go for the experience, you're headed for destruction.

ROADKILL

My son, Josiah, always wants to go where he is forbidden—the street in front of our home. He can play anywhere he wants to in our yard and even in our neighbors' yards. But the one place he thinks will bring him the ultimate fun is the place where he is forbidden, the street.

Out of my deep care for his health, his joy, his future, I warn him away from the street. I command him not to get near the street. I explain the consequences of what playing in the street could bring him. I threaten him with discipline if he ignores me. I do this out of my intense love for him as my son. I kneel down, look him in the eye, point to the street, and say, "Hey buddy, look at Daddy. Look in Daddy's eyes. Daddy's not playing around right now. You are never, *ever*, to go near that street. You can get bad 'boo-boos.' You can get hurt in that street, son. You can lose your life in that street. It would break Daddy's heart for you to go onto that street and something happen to you. It will upset Daddy if you disobey. Daddy will spank your hiney if you do. Stay away from the street."

The experience of sexual sin can be seductive. You can convince yourself it's not hurting anyone, no one will know, it's just one time, and so forth. You can rationalize what God has declared and commanded about the facts that sexual sin can ruin you, and go for the experience. But the experience could make you "roadkill" on the street of sexual sin. Trusting the sexual facts God has laid out about sexual sin will guard you. Ignoring and rationalizing the facts and going for the sexual experience will destroy you. Treasure the facts of God and the commands of God. "Obey them and live!"[4]

NOTE TO SELF

Solomon points out the window and said: "I was looking out the window of my house one day and saw a simple-minded young man who lacked common sense."[5] In other words, Solomon watched the unfolding of a young man who would ruin his life. And he took mental notes. He watched and applied the gravity of the young man's destruction and passed it along to us.

Like Solomon, take note of lessons from life. What lessons have you learned about what adultery can do to a family, the impact of pornography on a mind, the regret of premarital sex by a young person? Here are a couple of lessons I've observed and learned.

ADULTERY IS LIKE A DEATH IN THE FAMILY

I have a friend whose dad confessed to an adulteress affair. It was my friend's junior year of college. He was 21 years old. His dad called him at school and told him to come home. He thought someone had died. When he arrived home he walked inside and discovered his mom sitting in a chair, hand with Kleenex* over her mouth, sobbing. He asked her, "Who died?" She replied, "No one, but it sure feels like someone did." He walked outside where his dad was sitting on the porch steps. It was there that his dad tearfully, ashamedly, and penitently, shared the news. Later his dad packed up his clothes and headed for a local hotel. My 21-year-old friend stood at the living room window, hands on the glass, sobbing like a baby.

I observed that the grief of adultery is almost as intense as the grief of losing a loved one to death. And this includes the family as a whole, not just the spouse who was betrayed. I've observed that even one who is repentant of the adultery still carries near unquenchable guilt and shame. This sounds simplistic but the lesson is so obvious: I've learned that I never want to put my wife and kids, nor myself, through that. Ever.

PORN WARPS

I was pretty much forced into having an accountability partner in seminary. My accountability partner especially dreaded the "lust" question. It led down a deeper pathway to the major issue in his life. He shared it with me during our second meeting together. He was a porn addict. He had been since he was a teenager and he was now 40 years old. He reeked of shame. He wouldn't look me in the eye. He begged for my help and pleaded with me to hold him accountable not to do it.

A couple of weeks later I reluctantly brought it up. He actually snapped at me. I was taken aback. He followed by barking he couldn't quit porn. It was his secret sin and no one knew but me. "Have you told anybody?" he asked. "Nah, bro. It's between you and me." But he stayed paranoid with me. He leaned in close and shared with me how people on his dorm hallway were whispering about him, then avoiding him, and so forth.

Granted, I don't know the whole story. But I can confidently say that there were most likely no guys whispering outside of my friend's dorm room. I believe porn had him by the throat in such a way that he was so guilt-ridden and poisoned by the images with which he saturated his mind that he was losing touch with reality.

Skimming through porn or saturating your mind in it can set you on a dark path. And the dark will get darker. I've been there and I still fight from going there. You can get lost in an addiction and not ever fully find your way out. Your mind can become warped and darkened. What you expose yourself to repeatedly can haunt you for the rest of your life.

These are the facts. A hot orange oven burns. Playing on a busy street kills. Sexual sin destroys. Will you learn from the facts or choose to go the way of experience? Trusting the facts can protect you. Trying the experience can ruin you.

INVENTORY

♦ Reread the underlined portions of Scripture at the beginning of this chapter. In place of the underlined phrases of the passages above, go back and plug in "premarital sex," or "adultery," or "homosexuality" or "pornography." How do these texts impact you?

♦ Why do you think adultery can feel like a loved one passed away? How does this reality speak to you and your life?

♦ Although God, through Solomon, has given us the facts about the cost of sexual sin, why are we so tempted to go for the experience?

♦ In what ways can porn ruin your mind? How could it haunt you for the rest of your life?

♦ List three things that you can do today to protect yourself from experiencing sexual sin.

TIP #9

LIVE IN DENIAL

He was going down to the street near her corner, walking along in the
direction of her house at twilight, as the day was fading, as the dark of night set in.

- PROVERBS 7:9

With persuasive words she led him astray; she seduced
him with her smooth talk.

- PROVERBS 7:21

"Do not let your heart turn to her ways or stray to her paths.
many are the victims she has brought down....

- PROVERBS 7:25-26

The U.S. Chief of Naval Operations released a transcript of a conversation that took place with Canadian authorities off the coast of Newfoundland in 1995. The conversation is as follows:

Americans: "Please divert your course 15 degrees to the north to avoid a collision."

Canadians: "We recommend you divert your course 15 degrees to the south to avert a collision."

Americans: "This is the captain of a U.S. naval ship. I say again, divert your course."

Canadians: "No, I say again, divert your course."

Americans: "This is the aircraft carrier *USS Missouri*. We are a large warship of the U.S. Navy. Divert your course now!"

Canadians: "This is a lighthouse. Your call."[1]

Too bad this isn't a true story because, number one, it's hilarious.[2] Number two, it teaches a strong lesson. Still, we can apply the lesson. If we took the story at face value, we'd agree that disaster was certain if the ship didn't divert its course. The captain would have been stupid not to. Yet that is how many choose to live their lives in the face of sexual temptation. How far is too far; how long can I look; how much can I get away with? Or, the belief that all is under control; it's not hurting anyone; the temptations will never become reality; porn is just looking at the menu and not eating from it. This is flat out denial. And living in denial will ruin your life.

PERMISSION TO SIN

We can rationalize anything, especially when we feel beat up. Sexual fantasies and possibilities numb our mind to dealing with our own issues. It's there we find escape, relief, and a type of self-medication. Shanuti Feldhahn, in her book, *For Women Only: What You Need to Know about the Inner Lives of Men*, pegged where men are their most vulnerable to sexual sin. I know it's interesting that I refer to a woman's book to illustrate how we tick, but she really nails it. She probably knows men better than most know themselves. She mentions the HALT principle.

H = Hungry
A = Angry
L = Lonely
T = Tired

These frames of mind and body can sneak up on us. If we nurse them or deny them, we'll find it easier to rationalize sexual temptation. In addition, we'll default to walking a little closer in immorality's direction. Feldhahn states,

> If a man is working long hours, is out of sorts with the world (or his spouse), feels under appreciated, feels like a failure as a provider, or is far from home on a business trip—any or all of these things can weaken his resolve.[3]

We can't deny the very issues that will weaken us spiritually and morally. Indeed, half the battle is recognizing when we slip into the hunger, anger, loneliness, or fatigue mode.

HUNGRY

My pastor shared with me a truth I've never forgotten. "Unless your heart is satisfied, you will eat. Immorality is born out of hunger." Just take a look at Esau. Esau went out on an all-day hunt. He came home famished. Jacob had just cooked a pot of stew.

> Esau said to Jacob, 'I'm starved! Give me some of that red stew.' Jacob replied, 'All right, but trade me your birthright for it.' 'Look I'm dying of starvation!' said Esau. 'What good is my birthright to me now?' So Jacob insisted, 'Well then, swear to me right now that it is mine.' So Esau swore with an oath, thereby selling all his rights as the firstborn to his brother. Then Jacob gave Esau some bread and lentil stew. Esau ate and drank and went on about his business, indifferent to the fact that he had given up his birthright.[4]

The author of Hebrews tied the episode to our lives: "Make sure that no one is immoral or godless like Esau. He traded his birthright as the oldest son for a single meal. And afterward, when he wanted his father's blessing, he was rejected. It was too late for repentance, even though he wept bitter tears."[5]

Esau became consumed by his hunger and it cost him everything. He took advantage of a quick fix, an escape, and an instant pleasure. He lost the most precious and prized gift he could have received in his lifetime—the blessing and inheritance of his father. The point is that if your heart is not satisfied, you will find a quick something or someone to satisfy it, or at the least relieve it. And that quick fix can devastate your life. Don't live in denial of a "hungry" heart.

Here is a profound slice of truth: "Honey seems tasteless to a person who is full, but even bitter food tastes sweet to the hungry."[6] A few realities to consider here: The things of God (His Word, obedience, close relationship with Him) become unattractive to the man who gorges on sexual sin. In addition, a man's own wife can become "unattractive" because he is seeking his fill at sexual immorality's buffet. A man's sexual appetite will never be satisfied no matter how much, how often, or how long he gorges. *All* opportunities look attractive to him no matter how irrational. Just look at the man who committed adultery with a woman much less attractive than his own wife.

Don't deny when you get "hungry." Of course, we're not talking about hunger for food (although there could be argument for this as well), but hunger to be satisfied outside of God. That hunger can consume you. And the measures you take to satisfy that hunger through sexual sin can overwhelm you. Satisfaction and fulfillment can be satisfied in Christ alone. Think about it: you don't sin to feel worse, but to feel satisfied. To find satisfaction in a quick fix of sexual sin can cost you everything.

ANGRY

Anger can bring about a slow ruin. The apostle James says, "[D]on't sin by letting anger gain control over you. Don't let the sun go down while you are angry for anger gives a mighty foothold to the devil."[7] Anger in and of itself is not the issue. There is a righteous anger, such as when you get the wrong mobile telephone bill of $500 for the sixth month in a row and you're now on your 18th call to work it out. The anger I'm suggesting here is relational anger ignored and denied. This anger is like a dagger. It pierces your heart. The dagger wounds you deeply but doesn't kill you. It's left jabbed in your heart. The wound bleeds out. Sometimes the blood gushes, sometimes it trickles. But the pain is there and the wound constantly bleeds.

I argue that denying the deep-seated dagger of anger can lead to immorality. Whether you are single or married, this danger is real.

Anger inside of you from a past relationship gone sour or a rough childhood relationship with a parent or parents (or lack of relationship) can poison your spirit like a staph infection. Anger not recognized or addressed can skew your view of life. The wound from the dagger can hurt and bleed out to distract to the point that you make wrong decisions that poison relationships and lead you toward sexual sin.

Disillusionment with relationships, opportunities, and life in general can brood anger. You may have some serious baggage toward your father that you have denied or failed to consider. This will eat you alive. It will fuel the fire until you deal with it. Get help. Don't go through life angry with God and the world (although you may never admit to it or think of it in that way). That anger can prevent you from joy, and push you toward misery. And one way among many to attempt to relieve that misery is through sexual sin.

Everything in life may seem to work out wrong for you. Life hasn't been fair, you may say. Maybe you have sought applause, attention, achievement, and yet have always come up short. Or you have accomplished much but still remain dissatisfied. Either way, this broods an aching anger within you. That's what self-pity and unrelenting dissatisfaction do. Don't make yourself out to be a victim. Don't think you deserve more. You don't.[8]

Also, a word for the overachiever—you will never be satisfied. It's time to quit living on "happiness" and the high of beating the competition. Jesus is the only contentment.[9] He is the only One who gives life to the full.[10] Christ Jesus is your complete joy and satisfaction. Any "joy" or "satisfaction" found in sexual sin is cheap and fleeting.

On another note, past relationships with girls may have been dismal failures. You don't know if something is wrong with you or with them. I went through that dilemma when I was single. You're disillusioned and embittered toward girls and relationships, though you may fail to see it or admit it. Girls can quickly become objects of lust instead of sisters in Christ at this point. If you can't get anywhere relationally with a girl you might seek to fill that void and frustration through sexual sin.

If you've had many relationships fizzle or crash, or if you have barely had a relationship with a girl (but you have desired the companionship), the problem is most likely you, not the girl. You need to ask some honest questions about yourself. You need to pursue feedback from brothers and sisters in Christ about what relational and social "hang-ups" they may see in you. Do the hard work, as humbling and humiliating as it might be, to get to the root of what's going on with you. Don't take the easy way out through sexual sin.

For those who are married, you probably know that unresolved conflict between you and your spouse at bedtime gives the enemy an open door to mess with your affections and emotions.

Frustration can smolder if your wife is unavailable and insensitive to your sexual needs. This frustration can plant and grow a seed of bitterness. In that place you can rationalize and justify sexual sin. Be aware of this frustration and bitterness. Anger lurks within it. Be alert for the growing seed of bitterness and temptation to justify pursuit of sexual sin. Continually bring this anger and frustration before the Lord in prayer. Vent to a brother in Christ who will hold you accountable, bring perspective, and counsel you in the frustrations. Deny your fears and ego then, and respectfully and sincerely, share with your wife your struggle. Offer to take the lead in pursuing professional Christian counseling. Either way, do not ignore the anger, bitterness, and frustration.

LONELY

The human soul can't handle loneliness. Loneliness usually leads to isolation. Isolation always leads to loneliness. We weren't created for isolation but relationship with God and others. Loneliness and isolation therefore are a lethal combination.[11]

Isolated loneliness brings what my pastor calls, "justified self-centeredness." Key terms would be "nobody wants me." This is where the attraction of pornography can be most potent. Pornography displays the illusion to the viewer that he is wanted. It's the only time and place he feels wanted. He's convinced himself that he is the victim of his circumstances, failed relationships, and/or lack of relationships. So he retreats to find escape. He chooses loneliness. In that isolated loneliness he justifies the pursuit of sexual immorality.

On the other hand, you don't have to be isolated to be lonely. You can be the life of the party, the friend everyone comes to for counsel, an overachiever, an over-the-top-extrovert, but feel dreadfully alone. You can always have a smile on your face; you can have pep in your step. When asked how you're doing, you give a spiritually flavored answer. Yet your heart is distant, isolated, and empty.

Truth is that no human relationship can *ultimately* meet you in a way that totally extinguishes your loneliness. Only Christ can meet you in that desperate place. King David cries out to God, "Turn to me and have mercy on me, for I am alone . . .".[12] King David is not pleading with his wife or talking to a mirror. King David, the one who killed bears and giants and conquered nations, admits and cries out to God that he's lonely. Again, half the battle is recognizing that you are alone and isolated. It's confronting and dealing with that loneliness in your gut as you do your life. You confront it and deal with it by bringing it before Jesus.

God has given us friends to help us in the journey too. Though only Christ can meet us in the neediest place, He's given us relationships with people to meet deep needs within us also. Friends are a gift—"A friend loves at all times."[13] You need friends with whom you do life. True God-given, vulnerable, honest, relationships with brothers in Christ can be God-given antidotes to loneliness. But you have to work at being real and vulnerable. Working at those relationships is crucial. They don't come easy. Having a friend who asks you the tough questions and fosters out of you honesty about your state of mind and heart is priceless.

TIRED

When I'm tired, I'm tempted. There is no greater time that I want to escape and release than when I'm exhausted. I want to crawl on the couch with a bag of peanut M&Ms in one hand, a 16-ounce Coke in the other hand, and just disappear. Christie knows there is something wrong with me when I come home with a book, a *Newsweek* magazine, a *Time* magazine, a *Sports Illustrated* magazine, the *New York Times*, *USA Today*, and a stack of DVDs. She knows I want to escape and self-medicate. On the road when I arrive at my hotel room after a long day of speaking at schools, churches, or conferences, I want to crawl in the bed, flip on the tube, and channel surf. Inevitably when I do turn on the TV, the first option I have is to purchase a movie. One set of movies I can choose from is porn. I am most tempted at these moments of exhaustion even if I've spoken against porn and other sexual sin all day.

Gaining victory against ruin is to recognize when fatigue has you in a headlock. You don't keep fighting against the fatigue. You cry "uncle," and go get some rest. I don't know about you, but I am reluctant to give in to fatigue, much less cry "uncle" about it.

In his book, *The Rest of God*, Mark Buchanan talks about our need, and God's gift of Sabbath rest. He's not talking about Sundays. Buchanan is talking about a time when we put the work down even if it's unfinished. In relating the pressures of getting work done to the taskmasters of Egypt upon the Israelites, Buchanan writes:

> What God cares about, and deeply, is our needs. And it's this simple: you and I have an inescapable need for rest.
>
> The lie the taskmasters want you to swallow is that you cannot rest until your work's all done, and done better than you're currently doing it. But the truth is, the work's never done, and never done quite right.
>
> So what? Get this straight: The rest of God—the rest God gladly gives so that we might discover that part of God we're missing—is not a reward for finishing. It's not a bonus for work well done.

It's a sheer gift. It is a stop-work order in the midst of work that's never complete, never polished. Sabbath is not the bread we're allotted at the tail end of completing all our tasks and chores, the fulfillment of all our obligations. It's the rest we take smack-dab in the middle of them, without apology, without guilt, and for no better reason than God told us we could.[14]

Don't take exhaustion lightly. It could be a death-knell for you. It clouds your thinking. It makes you long for escape. It can cause your heart to "turn to [immorality's] ways or stray to her paths."[15]

If HALT has you "going down to the street near her corner, [and] walking along in the direction of her house,"[16] I'm calling you to divert your course. Recognize and deal with your hunger, anger, loneliness, and fatigue before immorality "leads you astray and seduces you with smooth talk."[17] If not, you'll remain on a collision course with ruin. But, it's your call.

INVENTORY

◆ Where are you seeking to fill your heart's hunger right now? What must you fill your life with instead? What will satisfy your soul? (Hint: Psalm 1).

◆ What has you angry right now? What anger from your past are you not dealing with? What is the danger of harboring this anger? How can you defeat this anger or keep it at bay?

◆ Are you lonely? What can you do about it?

◆ Does fatigue have you in its grip? Are you taking a Sabbath day to rest and play? Why or why not?

◆ Will you be brave enough to walk away from your work for a day of rest even though it's unfinished and unpolished?

TIP #10

DENY THE OBVIOUS

The woman approached him, dressed seductively and sly of heart.
She was the brash, rebellious type, who never stays at home.
She threw her arms around him and kissed him . . . .
My bed is spread with colored sheets of finest linen imported form Egypt.

- PROVERBS 7:10, 13, 16

A couple of years ago Christie, Josiah, and I visited her brother and his family in Minnetonka, Minnesota. It was during the month of December and freezing. Lake Minnetonka was frozen. Her brother wanted to take me on an ice fishing expedition on the lake. I was game ... kind of.

We walked out onto the ice. With every step I could hear the ice crackling and splitting beneath my feet. It wasn't encouraging.

Hundreds of feet offshore, we set up in an ice fishing tent. Inside he drilled holes about the size of small pizzas to drop our fishing lines into. He also placed a kerosene heater inside the tent with us and fired it up. This was a bit troubling to me, being that I had a deeply held belief that fire melted ice.

Due to the kerosene heater, the ice underneath us became mushier and mushier. I honestly don't think he noticed. And I didn't mention it. But what

I did mention was Jesus. He tends to come up in situations like this.

We made it home that afternoon without incident. I skimmed over their local newspaper to get a feel about what was happening in their community. On the front-page was a car that had fallen through the ice on one of the frozen lakes in the area. You can actually drive cars out onto the lake's ice at a certain point in the year. Obviously, it wasn't that time of year.

I studied the picture in disbelief. The front of the car was sunk. The trunk protruded out of the water. Then something caught my eye. In the front right corner of the picture was a sign that stood at the shore of the lake. No one could have missed it. The sign read, "Thin Ice."

The sign displayed the obvious. The ice was thin on the lake. You had the choice to enter at your own risk but the implication was you'd better not. There was a warning posted to ward off potential disaster. This particular driver denied the obvious and he paid the price.

Again, Solomon speaks of the immoral woman. Through his observations he turns and posts "thin ice" signs. He sounds warnings of sexual immorality's seduction. He's drilling danger signs into the ground about sexual immorality's ways.

Notice the words he uses to describe the immoral woman. Each word is like a warning sign of the kind of woman to run from. He said that she was "brash" and "sly."[1] She "dressed seductively."[2] When you put these words together with the rest of Proverbs 7, there is no denying the obvious. Consider some of these "thin ice" signs for sexual immorality:

- She comes on strong. (*Aggressive*)
- She's manipulative. (*Manipulative*)
- She dresses scandalously. (*Scandalous*)
- She's flirtatious, inviting, and easy. (*Seductive*)

AGGRESSIVE AND MANIPULATIVE

Met any aggressive and manipulative girls? If not, I assure you they're out there. And these types of girls are increasing all the more and becoming bolder. I wager that the time will come when this kind of girl will enter into your life. Guaranteed her aggression will take you off guard. You will be curious. But this is not the kind of girl you want anywhere near you. Often the guy who pursues or embraces this kind of gal fails to see the red flags about her. But his friends always can. Are you this guy? All you have to do is ask your friends for their point of view about her and you'll most likely see the flags you've missed or denied. Then you have to heed their words and counsel. I've been that guy who liked and dated that kind of gal. I got words, warnings, and counsel. But I refused to see. In the end, it cost me relationally, emotionally, financially, and spiritually

Take heed of the red flags. Abandon the relationship. Don't become her friend. And for crying-out-loud, don't twist it spiritually and be a "dating evangelist" or "Christian friend" to try to help her or "save" her. The odds are against you. Am I being too harsh? Read Proverbs 7.

She's not the kind of girl you want to take home to momma either. This is not the kind of lady you want to date, marry, or call "friend." She just isn't. If she comes on to you through text messages, e-mails, telephone calls, notes, words, and questionably innocent "affection," you'd better get off the ice quick. Cut all ties. If you are married, show your wife what she's sending you. Get serious, determined, and creative in ways to avoid and ignore her. Tell a brother in Christ about it so he'll check up on you. Have your friends, your small group, even your wife pray for her. She is a hurting soul, and expressing it in a sinful way. She needs Jesus.

Among various passing encounters through the years, one comes to mind immediately. I met an attractive girl on an airplane years ago and neither one of us wore wedding rings. I was single at the time and believed she was single. We chatted while in the terminal. After boarding the plane we actually ended up sitting together. I thought, *This is meant to be!* She gave me her number to look her up when I was back in town. I took this innocently because I told her I was a minister. Right before we parted ways she smiled, and said, "I'm going through a divorce. Call me." Without going into all the details leading to that moment, I'll just tell you that it became obvious what she wanted.

I met up with a buddy and told him the story. I told him how much I wanted to call her and stay in touch. I confessed my temptations to him. He prayed with me. He told me I needed to walk away and not look back. He held out his hand and I handed him her contact information. He ripped it up in front of me. I never looked back, and couldn't even if I wanted. Praise God.

I can't help but wonder how many guys come across aggressive, manipulative types of girls in their lives. Is it a common occurrence? I'm not one to say, but due to what reality shows and sitcoms display as normal, I again suggest that girls are becoming more and more aggressive sexually. I speak to teenagers. I have single friends. I hear the stories. So, caution. The potential for these encounters is increasing. It may not happen in high school but it could happen in the second year of your marriage, the fourth year of your career, or in the middle of a growing ministry.

SCANDALOUS AND SEDUCTIVE

She's dressed scandalously and seductively. Sometimes sin doesn't hide itself at all. It has the neon sign that says, "Come and enjoy." And we are strangely attracted to it. We lose touch with reality in a sense. It can launch us into sexual fantasies. Worse, that trigger of the flesh can overcome our rationale to where we might try and act on that lust and fantasy, if not with that type of woman, then through an outlet—such as porn.

You can tell much about a girl by the way she dresses. Some girls dress a bit sketchy because they think it looks cute. Others dress scandalously because they want you to want them. Either way, you don't need a talent for discernment to recognize that some women leave no doubt to what they want or what they want for you to want, simply by the way they dress and/or act. They are purposely scandalous and seductive. Take heed and stay off the ice.

SEXUAL SENSES

Immorality can appeal to our senses. I'll mention one that Solomon spotlights in Proverbs 7—our eyes.

Sexual immorality appeals to our eyes. The immoral woman dressed seductively, but she also "spread [her bed] with colored sheets of finest linen imported from Egypt."[3] It was an enticing view to behold. She is giving him a visual of the possibilities. She's offering him her "best." She's inviting him for the time of his life. She's showing him an intimate setting where his wildest dreams can come true. She doesn't have to say all those things. He only has to *see* her and what she offers, and his mind takes over.

When I think of the impact of sexual immorality visually I again think of porn. Truth is we don't have to take it as far as porn. Popular culture itself preys upon our eyes through common avenues such as TV commercials. I'll briefly mention one—a commercial for cologne. In the commercial a young man sprays on the cologne. Immediately afterward, attractive young girls dressed in school uniforms—with high skirts—mob him. The insinuation is that beautiful girls are desperate to have sex with us if we wear the cologne. Personally, I don't think the commercial makes guys want to elbow their way through Wal-Mart in a mad rush for the cologne. On the other hand, the desire for a sexual encounter with a girl in school uniform can be birthed and/or fostered by way of fantasy or reality. And it all stemmed from what we witnessed on a prime-time commercial.

We all face sexual imagery that we don't ask for. Although sexual imagery finds its way into our eyes, we can still beat down the thoughts that follow with the truth of Scripture. Be critical of everything that comes into your eyes that stirs your testosterone. When overt sexual temptation or immorality props itself before you and opens the door to you, turn your face and walk away. Repeat to yourself: "Lust never satisfies." Sexual immorality will cost you. Don't deny the obvious.

PIECE OF CAKE

Years ago I was speaking at a Wednesday night youth outreach service. To drive home the theme of the night, I asked one of the ladies of our church to bake a huge chocolate cake. She put different colored icing over it as well to make it stand out all the more. It looked and smelled irresistible. I placed the cake in front of the platform and placed a rope around it and appointed guards there to keep the teenagers away.

During my message I kept pointing to the cake. I would ask again and again, "Doesn't this cake look goooood? Can you smell it? Smells goooood. Who wants some chocolate cake?" Everybody, especially the fellas, whooped wildly.

At the end of my talk I asked if they were ready for some chocolate cake. They all cheered. I said, "Well, let me go ahead and cut it and you can come and get it." As the single spotlight shone down, I cut into the middle of the cake and pulled it apart. To their shock and horror, throughout the cake were razor blades. Dozens of them. The spotlight hit the cake just right. The silver flickered in the light. Point made. You could hear the gasp all over the room.

My point was that no matter how good sin looked, how inviting it seemed, or how sweet it smelled, it could cost you dearly. You may think you've gotten away with it, yet the sin will be slicing and dicing your life.

Solomon in Proverbs 7 has cut the cake. He has showed you the enticement of it and displayed the razor blades. She, sexual immorality, can look good, smell good, and talk smooth, but she will slice you up and cut you down.

The chocolate cake had no warning signs of danger. But sexual immorality does, personally placed there in Proverbs 7 by God through Solomon. Only a fool would knowingly eat something with razor blades. Only a fool would dive into sexual sin knowing that it would ruin his life.

THIN ICE

Speaking of fools, I think it would be foolish to walk or drive a car onto a lake with a "thin ice" sign posted. But ice can be deceiving, particularly if there are other people who have ignored the warning signs and traveled on and off the ice apparently without incident. You can feel the same about sexual sin. Culture itself portrays people getting away with sexual sin without paying a price. Sexual immorality is often depicted as trendy, hip, and "normal." But what culture doesn't show are the emotional, relational, and most likely physical consequences of immorality years down the road. Regardless, the warning sign is still there and the danger remains true. To deny the obvious cost is venturing out onto thin ice. You never know when you will crash through. But I'm wagering you will.

Stay off the ice. Stay out of ruin.

INVENTORY

◆ For the more mature men, would you agree that girls are more sexually aggressive today than ever? Why or why not?

◆ How would you handle a woman's sexual advances?

◆ Does the way girls dress affect you? How? What can you do in response?

◆ What are some TV sitcoms that suggest that there is no real cost to sexual immorality? Do they influence you?

◆ Are you walking on "thin ice?" Where has God posted signs in your life?

TIP #11

BE GULLIBLE

She threw her arms around him and kissed him, and with a brazen look
she said, "I've offered my sacrifices and just finished my vows."
"Come, let's drink our fill of love until morn-
ing. Let's enjoy each other's caresses."

- Proverbs 7:13 - 18

t happened on April Fool's day my eighth grade year of middle school. Before school most of my friends would hang out by the outside doors of the gym. As I was walking toward my posse, they were all chuckling and looking at me. My first thought was "zip up." But all was well there. I walked up to them and said, "What's up? What's so funny?" My best friend Lance pulled out from behind his back an egg. He slammed it onto my head. I stood in shock. I leaned my head over to catch the egg goop as it ran off my head. But there was no goop. Lance had pulled a glorious April Fool's joke on me. The egg was boiled.

Once I shook off my instinct to pummel him, I laughed and thought it was the funniest thing ever. Then he took out another egg. I was putty in his hands. I said, "Let me get somebody." He gladly handed over the egg.

I was waiting for my other friends to come by but none ever showed.

The first warning bell rang. I didn't want to miss out on the prank. I had to pull it on somebody pronto. Most everyone had made their way to class except me, Lance, and three or four of our friends. The last kid to walk toward the door was a sixth grader hobbling on crutches and barely hanging on to his books under his arms.

I walked up to him and said, "Hey, would you like an egg?" Then I slammed the egg on top of his head just like Lance did me. Problem: This was a raw egg.

As the egg yoke ran down his face he looked at me in horror. I was speechless. I spun around and Lance was foaming at the mouth he was laughing so hard. My friends had taken off running trying to contain themselves. I chased Lance around the building as the final bell rang.

Out of breath I decided to simply go surrender myself to the principal and accept my fate. Consequences were inevitable. I walked into his office and confessed the whole thing. As my story unfolded, it was all my principal could do to suppress his laughter.

Surprisingly the kid had yet to come to the office. I had a hunch he was in the hall bathroom by the office. Sure enough there he stood propped on his crutches swishing water over his face and head. I felt so ashamed. You should have seen me wetting paper towels and helping him clean egg off his face while he slapped at my hand as if it were a gnat. I rambled on about how Lance had set me up, that he (the kid) was my last chance to pull the prank, and so forth. I told him I'd be his body guard the rest of the year. He looked at me with fire in his eyes. You couldn't blame him.

Unfortunately, I'm still just as gullible. Pranks pulled on me aren't a difficult task. Actually, I think fewer pranks are pulled on me now because it's just plain boring. I'm too gullible, too easy a target.

NAÏVE AND MARRIED

It's one thing to be an easy target for innocent pranks. It is an entirely different issue to be gullible in sexual temptation. Upon further thought, gullible may be too soft a word. Naïve is more like it. To commend your emotions and issues to a woman outside of your marriage is a travesty. To entrust your heart and purity to just any woman before marriage can bring brokenness and regret. It's plain naïve.

In view of a friendship with a woman outside of marriage, my pastor told me that he refuses to be friends with women. It's not that he isn't cordial and compassionate. When called upon, he'll counsel a lady but it's always from behind a physical and emotional desk. He guards himself against gullibility and naiveté.

If you are married as I am, you have to take this seriously. If we are open to emotional friendships or ignorant of the possibility that friendships with women can evolve emotionally and then into something more, we are fools. These "friendships" are a recipe for ruin.

The wives of my close buddies are my friends for sure. My wife is friends with my buddies. But there are boundaries. Group friendship and fellowship is the goal and key. Conversations are always public. Any deeper-level conversation happens from couple to couple, not person to person. I am never alone with their wives in a car, house, or room. Neither are they with my wife.

I don't ride in cars alone with a woman. When I am picked up from an airport, or driven from venue to venue, the woman must have another person in the car with her. There have been exceptions in the past, I admit, due to unforseen circumstances out of my control. The entire time I was uncomfortable, cautious, and even stated my discomfort. Still I do everything in my power to prevent these situations.

Also, I have female friends with whom I talk about ministry and partner with in ministry. But emotions are caged and conversation public. Christie sees all my text messages. She checks my e-mails for me. If ministry circumstances caused me to me to be in a car alone with a woman, I tell Christie and my staff about it. I share with her about all my conversations. Christie is my partner in all the ministries to which God has called me.

In addition, you will never hear personal conversations between me and another woman, whether she is married or single, young or old, about any of her or my personal issues. If you're married, neither should you make yourself open to those kind of conversations.

The above situations can open doors of potential temptaton, doors that should never be darkened. The apostle Paul says, "Marriage should be honored by all."[1] Honoring marriage means not to be gullible to the potential of sexual temptation. In other words, don't put yourself in situations and conversations that could look, feel, and become suspicious.

I have female friends that I once hung out with when I was single. I still get calls from them every now and then asking to meet for lunch to get caught up. If we meet up, it will be in public with another friend or two joining us. Or Christie and I have them over for lunch or dinner. The relationships have always been platonic mind you. I never dated these girls. I have no attraction to them now. And I imagine they don't have any attraction to me. But I'm not going to be gullible and naïve on possibilities that innocence can get sullied by me, or them. But even more importantly, I want to honor my wife and Jesus.

NAÏVE AND SINGLE

To be a young, single adult male who meets a girl and is immediately gripped by her sweet talk, or hot body, or cute charm, or even her spirituality, without getting to know what makes her tick, can devastate you. Your gullibility can blind your eyes and numb your senses to the possibilities of years of pain, deep regret, and difficult healing, not to mention the distance it would bring to your relationship with Jesus.

I was asked by a single guy a while back the following: "How can you know if the person you're dating will not become someone different after marriage?"

Scientifically speaking, according to Dr. Jay Giedd, chief of brain imaging in the child psychiatry branch at the National Institute of Mental Health, the estimated age for when the brain is fully mature is 25 years old.[2] This may be worth noting. The chances of your girlfriend changing, and you changing, for the better or worse, are greater under the age of 25. I know I was an entirely different person at age 25 than I was at age 21. Therefore, to marry under the age of 25 could be a risk. Of course, the age of 25 is not the magical age of maturity by any means. There are always risks. I know 18 year olds who are more mature than some 30 year olds. Simply take the data for what it's worth.

On another scale, ask yourself these questions: Think in patterns (which means you must take time to get to know the real her). How does she treat her parents? What are her friends like? There's an old proverb that reads, " If you want to know a [person's] character, just look at his or her friends."

Does she love Jesus with all of her DNA? Does she lie? Does she care about people? Pushing emotions aside the best you can, do you trust her with all of your heart? How does she use her money? If she has a career that keeps her on the road for weeks out of the year, would you completely trust her to be faithful? I am no expert. This is no exhaustive list, but it's a start.

DATING STANDARDS

A relationship has begun with you and a girl. You like her. She likes you. You both love Jesus. You are now boyfriend and girlfriend. We can take it further—let's say you are engaged. The standards are the same whether dating or engaged.

So what are your standards? They should be standards driven by the Scriptures. Here are three:

One, the apostle Paul says: "But among you there must not be even a hint of sexual immorality, or of any kind of impurity . . .."[3] The words "not even a hint" leave no wiggle room. Sexual petting of any sort, mutual masturbation, and any thing else you come up with is tagged by this text. Again, I like how pastor Mark Driscoll stated the following in a sermon series dealing with sex. He said the question is not, "Where's the line?" but, "When's the time?" Answer: marriage. The question isn't, "How far is too far?" but rather "How not to get going until you're married!" To even ask the questions about how far you can go sexually with your girlfriend exposes the sinful motives of your heart.

Two, King Solomon records the words of his soon-to-be bride: "Do not arouse or awaken love until it so desires."[4] The New Living translation says, "until the time is right." This text alone nails the sexual standard for a dating relationship. "Love" here is referring to sexual intimacy. So when is it the right time to sexually arouse? Marriage. When is the wrong time? Any time outside of marriage. God didn't give the gift of sexual arousal for us to slam the brakes on. He gave sexual arousal so we'd go all the way. Sexual arousal heightens the anticipation of "oneness" and pleasure within marriage.

Does "snuggling" arouse you or her? If you're not married, then the Scriptures say not to do it because arousal is happening. Does kissing arouse you or her? Then don't do it. I don't want to be legalistic but you have to guage yourself and the feelings of your girlfriend by the Scriptures. A simple kiss on the cheek, or a momentary kiss on the lips may be fine. Or it could potentially lead to arousal. If it leads to arousal, don't do it. What about holding hands? I'll just say this—if anything you do with your girlfriend arouses you, don't do it.

Sexual petting and any other degree of sexual behavior arouses and is declared by the Scriptures as *poreniea*, or immorality. Therefore, the Scriptures say, don't do it. All said and done, to be with your girlfriend in physical ways with the goal of putting the breaks on is foolish. The brakes will eventually fail altogether. Again, God never meant for a man and woman to hit the brakes when they are sexually aroused. He didn't wire us that way. God didn't design sex that way either. We're meant to go all the way. That's why He says not to arouse "before the time is right." The right time of sexual arousal is only in marriage. When sexually aroused in marriage, there are only green lights to go for it, not red lights to stomp the brakes.

Three, in 1 Timothy 5:2, the apostle Paul commands, "[Treat] older women as mothers, and younger women as sisters with absolute purity." In other words, your girlfriend, even girls in general, is to be treated like a sister until you are married. Think about that the next time you snuggle! Her purity, her life as a whole, is to be guarded, valued, and honored by you. She is your sister, not just your date. She is your sister, not just your girlfriend. She is your sister before she is your wife. This ought to tie up any loopholes that the sinful heart can find to rationalize sexual sin.

CHURCH SEX

In Proverbs 7, the immoral woman "threw her arms around him and kissed him, and with a brazen look she said, 'I've offered my sacrifices and just finished my vows.'"[5] Did you catch that element of spirituality? It was a spiritual custom in that day for the people of God to go to the priest with an animal sacrifice. The priest would place the offering on the altar and set it ablaze as worship. Then a portion of the meat would be given to the priest. The worshiper would take his or her portion of the prime rib home to eat as a celebration to God.

On the outside she was doing some good spiritual things. She was worshiping the Lord, so it seemed. Yet her behaviors betrayed her worship. This tinge of spirituality thrown in might have eased his conscience a tad too. After all, a worshiping woman can't be that bad, right? He was ridiculously naïve and gullible.

I, too, have been that naïve and gullible. When I was single, I spoke on summer mission trips around the world. I worked for a missions organization out of Atlanta, Georgia. Arriving at the mission site in Mexico on a Saturday afternoon, I was greeted by the summer missions staff. One girl in particular made her way right to me. And I was thrilled. She was attractive in every sense of the word.

We became inseparable. Every spare minute we had we hung out and took walks. One particular afternoon the mission groups were walking around an impoverished neighborhood to pray with families in their homes. This girl and I did our prayer walk together apart from the groups. That evening we were hanging around with other summer missions staff. One of the staff girls said to the girl to whom I'd been attached to the hip, "I bet you miss your husband. Is he going to be able to visit anytime this summer?"

I kid you not. I almost blacked out. I can't even recall her initial answer. I instinctively looked at her ring finger (as I had done when I first met her). Confirmed again. There was no wedding ring. But still I had been too gullible.

I immediately walked away from the conversation and her. I was literally freaked out. I avoided her like the plague the rest of the week. It felt awkward and looked awkward to everyone, I'm sure. I left at the end of the week in a daze without so much as an acknowledgement of her existence. I was completely at a loss.

That's not the end of it. Before I knew she was married, I had given her my e-mail address and mobile telephone number. She e-mailed and called me numerous times. She wanted advice about her marriage troubles. After weeks of avoiding her, I answered her call one day. I told her I couldn't help her. I encouraged her to to pursue Jesus, and to love, support, and stay committed to her husband, and to never contact me again. It ended that day.

Mind you, this same girl wore Christian t-shirts that week. She sang worship songs. She read her Bible. We even prayed together, for crying-out-loud. I learned my lesson that outward Christianity can be deceiving.

Don't be naïve. Sexual sin can be cloaked in Christian garb. You don't have to go to Las Vegas to happen upon sexual opportunities. It lurks in the church and missions organizations. The immoral woman can be raising her hands to "Here I Am to Worship." You can become an immoral man leading a Bible study every Tuesday night. Don't be naïve. Guard your life.

THE FALL OF THE CHRISTIAN

In over ten years of ministry I've witnessed many Christian young men and women stray from the Lord because of a dating relationship that became sexual. Indeed I believe that is one of the biggest downfalls of Christian young men and women.

First, there's the desire for a boyfried or girlfriend. A dating relationship begins. The relationship becomes an idol. Affections and emotions become so engaged that the Lord grows more and more distant from their hearts. It's like watching a slow death of spiritual love. Then most times the lines of sex are tip-toed and ultimately crossed. They disappear from the church. Though not always the case, it does seem to be a pattern. It breaks my heart.

Don't be that guy. Don't be gullible to a girl's spirituality without the test of time. On a stronger note, don't be the man who leads gullible women into your lusts, or to prove your manhood, or to fit in, or to boost your ego, or to see if "you've still got it."

Control yourself. "Be on the alert, stand firm in the faith. *act like men,* be strong."[6] Do so by the grace of God. Don't pull the strings of a girl's emotions. Don't befriend women outside of your marriage, particularly at emotional levels. And to use spirituality to get what you want out of a woman, whether sexually or otherwise, is evil. God will judge you.

NATURE OR NURTURE

Guard your godliness. Cherish your relationship with the Lord Jesus more than any woman. Beware of your affections and emotions for a girl who is slowly securing your heart and mind even if you think she's a "good Christian girl." Keep constant gauge on the nature of your relationship. A couple of good questions to ask: Are your affections and emotions being weaned away from Jesus by her? Are you becoming her-centered instead of Jesus-centered?

Do what you must do to stay Jesus-centered. This will guard your heart and give you wisdom. When I married Christie, one of my vows was to "love Jesus more than Christie so that I might love her better." You must always seek to love Jesus more.

Be a man. Be the leader in your relationship. Guard against slipping away from Jesus and the people of God and taking her along with you. Don't be gullible and naïve to the possibilities.

LESSONS FROM AN EGG

I still reflect on my ignorance and gullibility of taking a raw egg and crashing it on that poor kid's head. I think back at how I stood there with my mouth gaping, shocked at what I'd done. I remember looking down seeing broken shells in my hand and longing to change that moment.

Don't be sexually gullible and naïve. Beware of putting yourself or allowing yourself into a situation where you might one day say, "What have

I done? I would give anything to change this. I would give anything and everything to take it all back." It's one thing to see the shells of a broken egg in your hand. It's wholly unthinkable that out of sexual gullibility you could hold in your hand the shells of a ruined life.

INVENTORY

◆ What was the most impacting part of this chapter? Why?

◆ How would you define godliness? What would you say is the difference between "a great Christian guy" and a godly man? Which mold do you fit?

◆ For singles: What about a girl could bring "red flags" to you pursuing a relationship with her? What red flags do you recognize about yourself?

◆ For singles: What do you look for in a girl? What would you say the difference is between a "good Christian girl" and a "godly woman?"

◆ What boundaries do you need to establish with girls to prevent youself from being gullible? If you're single, what lines do you believe you should establish in dating a girl? If you are married, what lines do you need to draw with female friends and co-workers?

TIP #12

MAKE EXCUSES

She threw her arms around him and kissed him....

- Proverbs 7:13.

It's you I was looking for! I came out to find you, and here you are!

- Proverbs 7:15

Almost all college basketball teams view tape of the opposing team a week before the game. We were no different. We were playing Davidson College, out of Charlotte, North Carolina, on a Tuesday night. A week before the game our team watched taped segments of plays and players at the beginning of every practice for about 30 minutes to an hour. Then we went to the floor and rehearsed how to stop them. One particular play by Davidson involved an inbounds pass from under their goal. The play was geared toward Davidson's 6'10", 250-pound center. There would be screens set for his defender. Then the ball would be lobbed in the air near the basket for him to catch and dunk it. Guess who was guarding Davidson's center? Yours truly.

We rehearsed the play again and again by viewing tape, doing walk-throughs in practice, and a final walk-through the afternoon before the game. Our head coach, John Brady, (former head coach of the LSU Tigers, current head coach of Arkansas State), drilled me to be alert for the screen.

Davidson was strong. The game went back and forth until about half-way through the first half. Sure enough, Davidson got the ball under their goal. It was inevitable that it would happen. Coach Brady and the assistants were shouting at me to beware of the screens.

The player passing the ball inbounds slapped the ball to begin the play. And sure enough, I got pinned by the screens. As I saw Davidson's goliath turn the corner, I tried to fight through the screen. But it was too late. I looked up. The ball was in the air. I was staring at his waist. Then it happened: "boom!" He thundered the ball through the goal. I swear I felt the wind off it.

The Davidson students and fans absolutely lost their minds. I jogged back down the court while Coach Brady was losing his mind too. He stared me down. He walked past the scorer's table and ruthlessly let me have it. His screams were primal. I couldn't understand a word he was yelling because of the cry of the crowd's mocking. I just gazed at him and nodded in agreement with whatever. He could have been saying, "Jarrod, you're an orange," and I would have been agreeing wholeheartedly.

As I listened and watched the scream and dance of Coach Brady, I lost track of Davidson's center. Well, *he* found *me*. He had stepped out a quarter of the way up the court standing tall and hard like a 6'10" reinforced concrete wall. I didn't see him. With no warning I ran headfirst into him. I saw a bright flash of light. My ears rung. My vertebrae cracked from my neck down to my lower back. He was a wall. I just sort of melted to the floor and onto a knee.

I shook it off best I could. Even more humiliated, I looked over at Coach Brady who buried his face into his hands and shook his head in disbelief. It was not a good day. Things had gone from bad to worse. And it got even worse. I got pulled from the starting line-up the second half. And with the help of my questionable play the first half, we lost the game by over 20 points.

As I sat on the sidelines I thought of 20 excuses of how Davidson executed the inbounds dunk play perfectly. I had excuses of how I couldn't stop the play because I was illegally screened and held. But excuses would not be accepted even if I tried making a case. Excuses could not make up for the harm I caused in that game either. I knew their inbounds play. I just wasn't mentally prepared for it. I didn't take it seriously enough. I wasn't committed to fighting tooth and nail to stop it. I didn't make up my mind to give it everything I had until it was too late. I got comfortable. My preparation was not translated into action.

VIEWING TAPE

Proverbs 7 is like viewing tape of sexual ruin. We're seeing the plays of immorality unfolding before us. We're getting instructed and empowered. But we have to put the instruction into action. We better take this thing seriously. We better be mentally and emotionally prepared and resolved. We better be committed to fighting against temptation to the death. We can't wait until the last minute to make choices. Excuses and rationalization tend to win out at the last minute.

EXCUSES, EXCUSES

Sin and excuses have been around since the creation of man. God commanded Adam, "From any tree of the garden you may eat freely; but from the tree of the knowledge of good and evil you shall not eat, for in the day that you eat from it you will surely die."[1]

Then came "the serpent," Satan. He said to the woman, "Indeed, has God said, 'You shall not eat from any tree of the garden'?"[2] Instead of having driven the flag into the ground to trust the fact of God's command, they were unresolved. So they ate the fruit, and sinned.

Following their sin came the excuses. First, Adam: "The man said, 'The woman whom you gave to be with me, she gave me from the tree, and I ate'."[3] Then, Eve: "And the woman said, 'The serpent deceived me, and I ate'."[4] God's response was that the earth, nature, and humanity would be cursed with sin and death until Jesus came to conquer it through the Cross.[5]

Excuses can follow sin. Adam's excuse for sin? "… it was Eve's fault." On the other hand, sin can follow excuses. After listening to the serpent, Eve had her excuse for sin: "The fruit is there for the taking! It looks so good! How could I refuse when it's right there in front of me?" Sounds like a lot of guys I've known who've fallen to sexual sin—*How could I refuse?*

Either way, Adam and Eve sinned and excuses could not make up for it. They had paradise, protection, and a relationship with their Creator. God had made Himself clear that sin would cost them everything. Disobedience would ruin them and everything they knew to be good. And it did.

Excuses can follow sexual sin. Sexual sin can follow excuses. The Proverbs 7 young man could say, "You don't understand! She threw *her* arms around *me* and kissed *me*! She was there for the taking! How could I refuse? What could I do?" [6] Or, "She pursued *me*; she came looking for *me*, not the other way around! It wasn't all my fault." Or maybe, "I was lonely. She wanted me. I wanted her. I needed her. No one understands me like her."

I wonder if you have a girl like that in your workplace, a sister-sorority, in biology class, or at church. She makes you feel wanted. She gives you the vibe that she's available if you pushed the envelope. She's there for the taking. She's a peer, a co-worker, a friend. Perhaps she's just an acquaintance but she's sending you signals so clear that even you can't ignore the fact that she's interested in something more.

THE CATCH-22

Let's continue down this hypothetical road for a bit. You may be married and dealing with an aggressive woman. Or you may be single and dealing with a seductive woman. Whatever the case, she's flirting and the Holy Spirit has convicted you that you should avoid interest. He has made you uncomfortable about being around her. You've arrived to the point that you feel you must gently yet directly tell her to back off.

Prepare yourself. There is no way to "win" in this conversation. She'll ask, "Why?" No doubt she will be offended. Highly, highly offended. You'll probably get hammered with, "You're a jerk! Who do you think you are?

You're so arrogant." Don't be hurt. And don't take it personally. Take it on the chin like a man realizing that she'll probably tell all of her friends that you're a jerk.

I've heard of this scenario happening with other guys, multiple times. And I'd love to have a solution or a way to avoid this situation. If I could successfully come up with a solution and write it here, I'm sure I would make it into your T-Mobile's top five.

So what to do when you find yourself in this situation with a woman? Dismiss it? I would warn you not to dismiss it. That would be the easy way out of avoiding the above mentioned conflict. But that's dangerous. I say it's dangerous because keeping her "available" when you're not interested will eventually lead to a bigger conflict. Her advances will look enticing when you're lonely, or when your girlfriend breaks up with you, or you don't make the team, or your wife is not meeting your needs. It will be inviting even if you haven't been attracted to her. When your world gets shaken, perspectives and convictions can change on a dime, thanks to sin and the Enemy. Excuses can abound. I've been there. Sadly, in my younger days there were a couple of times when life got tough and I took advantage of an opportunity. I regret it. I wasn't following Christ at the time, but I admit that I wouldn't have had the courage to confront her anyway. Having Jesus as the Lord of your life will bring conviction and courage to have those gutsy conversations.

If you have that kind of woman around of you, you could be setting yourself up for ruin. Sure, it may sound like a bad idea to confront her because of the potential fallout. But how serious are you to not leave yourself open to any possibility of sexual sin, ruining your life, and breaking the heart of God? My pastor said we ought to put as many barriers between us and sexual temptation as possible. I'm fairly confident to say that if you confront a girl about her behavior around you or toward you as I described above, you can pretty much count her out of your life. That conversation becomes a monumental barrier.

In my opinion, most Christian single men, young and old, don't have an ambition for premarital sexual encounters. Likewise most married Christian men don't go looking for an adulterous relationship. If they do, that's a whole other subject. But there is still another particular way that you can leave yourself open to sexual sin.

SELF-PITY

So what might be one major lure to sexual sin that's not considered enough for us men? I believe it's what most guys would not admit to: self-pity.

I've touched on this in previous chapters but it bears repeating again and again for us guys. We are experts at making ourselves victims of our circumstances. We want to blame anything and/or anyone for our problems and brokenness. In so doing we become experts at rationalizing sin. Excuses come easy when we feel sorry for ourselves.

An injured ego makes a man particularly vulnerable. A woman can soothe in many ways. She can say things, do things, look at you in particular ways, laugh on cue, and so forth. It can start innocently enough, or like the immoral woman she could have had impure motives all along. Either way, when a woman strokes the ego, the doors of immoral possibilities begin creaking open. Fantasies are considered. Then the fantasy hints at possibilities, possibilities foster realities, and those realities bring ruin. James writes, "But each one is tempted when he is carried away and enticed by his own lust. Then when lust has conceived, it gives birth to sin; and when sin is accomplished, it brings forth death. Do not be deceived, my beloved brethren."[7] The New Living translation puts it this way: "Temptation comes from the lure of our own evil desires. These evil desires lead to evil actions, and evil actions lead to death. Don't be misled, my dear brothers and sisters."[8]

SEXUAL CLOUT

Consider again the Proverbs 7 encounter. She pursues the young man. She "*throws* her arms around him."[9] She embraces him. Then she slides her lips across his cheek to his lips. She kisses him slowly and passionately. She cups his face into her hands. Staring deep into his eyes, the warmth of her breath on him and smell of perfume around him, she says, "It's *you* I was looking for! I came out to find *you*, and here *you* are!" [10] He's primed to fall to her charm.

How could he refuse her in that moment? How could you or I? Imagine how his ego soared! He feels needed. He feels desired. He feels wanted. And his manhood is validated. What if he was going through a tough time in his life at that moment too? Envision the clout of her seduction had he been living a victim to brokenness and self-pity? Think about the power of her temptations if he was complacent, bored, or discouraged with his life or marriage. Imagine her grip on his sexual affections if he was depressed over not having a girlfriend or distraught at being single in his late 20s? Excuses for sex with her can abound.

OWN UP

Beware of becoming a victim in your own eyes. You must be man enough to own up to self-pity. You must reject vehemently any excuse to pursue sin of any sort because of what life has dealt you. I shared this verse in the last chapter, but I want to repeat it here: Paul said, "[S]tand firm in the faith, act like men, be strong."[11]

Most of us do a lousy job at handling life. We may have a veneer for everyone on the outside but inside we're a wreck. The danger, however, is failing to own up to this reality. If we finally do own up, the greater danger is not pleading our need to Jesus. The result is that sin happens and excuses follow, or excuses happen and sin follows.

Only Jesus, through the Holy Spirit, can give you grace to endure life's fallouts. He's the only way that your loneliness, brokenness, neediness, and disappointments can be relieved and removed from your life. Sexual sin is not relief. It's ruin.

NO EXCUSES

My team got butchered by Davidson College. I'm convinced they gained momentum immediately following the dunk on my head. It could be that my mistake began a sequence of events that ruined the game for us. Their momentum became too great to stop. None of my excuses made up for that. I did take responsibility, however, for that mistake. Though the loss was recorded forever, I hoped I'd get another chance to play against them. I wanted to prove myself to my coaches and teammates. To my regret, there wasn't another game. I never had another opportunity to make things right.

On a much deeper level, a sexual mistake can ruin you. Sin can bring excuses or excuses can bring sin. But excuses will never give you a free pass from the consequences. No matter how you try to rationalize sexual sin in your life, no excuse will save you. The loss can be forgiven but it will forever be recorded on your relational and emotional score sheet. The damage might never be undone. You might not get another chance to make things right. Only time and God's grace will tell.

Listen to the call of God through Proverbs 7. Listen to King Solomon jumping up and down on the sidelines of your life. Don't buy into the flattery. Don't make excuses for your sexual sin. You *will* get slammed on. You will lose.

INVENTORY

◆ How can Proverbs 7 prepare you mentally and emotionally to face sexual temptation?

◆ What does Scripture mean by "flattery"? How can that relate to you?

◆ What does the following mean: "Sexual sin can bring excuses. Excuses can bring sexual sin"? What excuses could one make to commit sexual sin?

◆ Where in your life have you felt "pummeled"? How did you handle it? Were you tempted to find pornographic (or other sexual means) escape? Did you find escape there? Explain.

TIP
#13

GET HARDENED
TO GOD'S TRUTH

My son, keep my words and treasure my commandments within you.

- PROVERBS 7:1

Even a serial killer reads his Bible.

Dennis Rader, the renowned "BTK" (Bind, Torture, Kill) serial killer was interviewed after his capture by a television newsmagazine. In the midst of the interview, BTK looked his interviewer square in the eye and said, "I read my Bible everyday." At the time of his capture he was also president of the church council at Christ Lutheran Church in Wichita, Kansas. Mind you, he was reading his Bible and serving his church while committing years of horrendous murder. Don't miss the point here. The issue is not that he was ignorant of God's Word. He was numb to it.

Beware. If someone can go through the motions of reading his Bible daily and become so hardened toward the truth that he would "bind, torture, and kill" people, we too are not exempt from reading the Scriptures and becoming hardened to the truth about sexual sin.

Proverbs 7 has been the writings of Solomon to his favorite son—

Rehoboam. However, the very words Solomon spoke to his son he failed to heed himself. Eventually, Solomon's heart was led astray from God. This paints a disturbing reality. The very convictions one has and the words one speaks against sexual sin and moral failure can be compromised and abandoned. No one is immune.

The book of Ecclesiastes reveals Solomon's demise. He didn't deny himself any pleasure, especially sexually. He had 700 wives, and 300 concubines.[1] All the sex he could stand. But he was left empty. "'Everything is meaningless,' says the Teacher, 'utterly meaningless'."[2] "'I said to myself, "Come, now let's give pleasure a try. Let's look for the good things in life. But I found that this, too, was meaningless'."[3] "[I] had many wonderful concubines. I had everything a man could desire."[4] "'[I]t was all so meaningless'."[5] You can sense the regret and sorrow in his words. The very truths he shared with his son he abandoned. It left him void and broken. How much more passionate would he be about Proverbs 7 now that he's on the other side? We've had much to learn through Solomon's wisdom and through his downfall.

However, we can't reflect on Proverbs 7 as the hypocritical words of a king gone astray. The truth is the truth. Sexual sin will ruin your life. So take to heart all that Solomon said. God, through Solomon, desired to relay life's grandest wisdom to save us from sexual ruin.

THE BEST FOR LAST

On a confessional note, I've saved the best chapter for last. The Scripture below this chapter's title is actually the words which began Proverbs 7. I'm thankful and relieved you have made it this far in the book. The truth of this chapter is where I find power not to ruin my life with sexual sin. The same will go for you. If you do not embrace the truths found in this chapter and put them into practice, then your victory over sexual sin will be impossible to sustain. I'd go so far to say that your fight will be in vain without the Scriptures. God's Word through the power of His Spirit and His Spirit through the power of His Word is your only hope.

CHEWING THE CUD

Solomon's words reveal the magnitude of what protects us from sexual sin. He pleads, "My son, *keep* my words and treasure my commandments within you. *Keep* my commandments and *[keep* my teachings]. . . ."[6] That's why he repeats the word "keep" like a broken record.

That being the case, the Scriptures are to be savored, not surfed. He says, "[keep] . . . and treasure my commandments within you . . . ."[7] There is much more to our reading of Scripture than just "reading" Scripture. I have a daily Bible reading plan that outlines what Bible texts I am to read for each day. It provides the chapters and verses from one of the Gospels, an Epistle (Paul's writings—Romans through Philemon (and possibly Hebrews but commentators differ on the authorship), a Psalm, and a Proverb. I feel very proud to see the checks beside each day of the month that I have finished my "assignment." But "checking off" my reading of God's Word can go from being a good thing to a bad thing. In my opinion, those checkmarks can become checkpoints of numbness to God's Word. For instance, I can read over daily verses or chapters to avoid guilt for not doing so whether I got anything out of it or not. I can also officially declare, "I had my quiet time with God" today. There's a sense of spiritual pride in that. In addition, there can be a hint of superstition in my reading over Scripture, such as thinking, *Since I read all those chapters, God is pleased and I'm going to have a good day.*

I admit that I've often approached Bible readings as a to-do list. I'm by nature a task person. I'm compelled to read that day's readings no matter how much it is. But Jesus talks about "abiding" in God's Word.[8] The psalmist deals with "meditating" on God's Word.[9] Just reading it is not enough.

An early church Father, St. Augustine of Hippo, used a metaphoric term for what I think he meant about abiding or meditating on Scripture. The term was "ruminate." Ruminate means to "chew the cud." Take a cow for example. A cow digests its food in two steps. First, it eats. Next, it regurgitates a partially-digested form of the food which is called cud. Then it continues eating by "chewing the cud." That whole process is what is called "ruminating."

According to studies, "dairy cows spend almost eight hours a day chewing their cuds for a total of almost 30,000 chews daily."[10] In addition, a cow gains between 50 percent to 70 percent of its energy by chewing the cud, or ruminating.[11] In application to us, constant daily reading *and* meditating on Scripture energizes and empowers us to beat sexual sin.

GETTING NOTHING OUT OF THE BIBLE

We are to "chew the cud" or "ruminate" on Scripture. The process of a cow chewing its cud is a picture of how we can understand the word "meditate" in the Bible. Psalm 1 begins with the words, "Blessed is the man . . ."[12] The man who is blessed is one who is not caught up in the affairs of sinful counsel, behavior, and belonging, but one whose "delight is in the law [the Scriptures] of the Lord, and on his law he *meditates* day and night."[13] Psalm 1:2 in *The Message* Bible says that you "thrill to God's Word, you *chew* on Scripture day and night."[14]

So what does this mean practically? Psalm 1:2 of *The Amplified Bible* helps us: "[H]is delight and desire are in the law of the Lord, and on His law (the precepts, the instructions, the teachings of God) he *habitually meditates (ponders and studies)* by day and by night."[15] Ruminating, chewing the cud, meditating, is not fitting in a quiet time with God so you can check off your day's Bible reading assignment. It's taking small chews and pondering them all day. This is ruminating on the Scripture. You are "chewing the cud."

You read to be transformed not informed. Informational reading is trying to cover as much of the Bible as possible, a Dennis Rader approach perhaps. But transformational reading is taking smaller chunks and reflecting on it. It's taking the time to allow a small section of Scripture probe you, master you, and shape you. "For the word of God is alive and powerful. It is sharper than the sharpest two-edged sword, cutting between soul and spirit, between joint and marrow. It exposes our innermost thoughts and desires."[16]

Read the text. Ponder, meditate, ruminate, chew on it. Pray it. Write it on an index card. Keep it in front of you throughout the day. Digest, or memorize it. Keep bringing it back up again and again to get all the nourishment you can from it. Let it intermingle with your thoughts, your desires, your hopes, your behavior, your regrets, your pain, your past. Let it argue with you. Read it out loud, one word at a time. Take note of the verb and nouns. Focus and concentrate. Dig in. The Holy Spirit will use this to energize and empower your obedience and protect you from ruin.

I had lunch with a friend the other day. He loves Jesus deeply but struggles with porn and other issues. He said, "I don't understand. I read my Bible every day. Sometimes I even read a whole book of the Bible but I just can't seem to get anything out of it." I told him, "Bro, you need to quit surfing and start savoring. You need to 'chew the cud'." The lights came on in his eyes. I hope it has for you as well.

WORTH IT

When you open the Scriptures, plead with God as did the psalmist: "Open my eyes to see the wonderful truth of your instructions."[17] Trust that His Word is perfect and trustworthy; it revives the soul, gives wisdom, brings joy to the heart, gives insight for living, fosters purity, and endures forever.[18] God's Word alone is worth the time and effort of your viewing, ruminating, and meditation. It pierces through your numbness to bring back feelings and desires for authentic holiness.

On a last note about "chewing the cud," it's interesting that a dairy nutritionist said,

> [A] content cow is one seen chewing her cud. . . . 60 to 70% of cows actually chew their cuds when they are resting. Pay attention to fresh cows to see that they are chewing their cuds. Taking time to carefully observe your cows will pay dividends in recognizing potential problems before they become major headaches.[19]

God's Word will bring contentment, rest, and relief. Sexual sin never will. Beware of getting numb to God's truth. Pay attention to whether you are surfing His Word or savoring it. His Word will pay huge dividends in your life. It will keep you alert to sexual temptation. It will prevent much more than "potential problems" and "major headaches." It will prevent you from ruining your life.

STREETWISE

King Solomon says, ". . . treasure my *commandments* within you. Keep my *commandments* . . ."[20] I know the power of God's Word. But I also know that my sinful, rebellious nature ruffles up at the word "commandments." It means that I'm being told what to do and not to do, where to go and not to go, how to act and not to act. But that's the point. I'm loved enough by God that I'm commanded not to ruin my life. I'm commanded to follow the path of life of the One in whose presence is the fullness of joy and in whose right hand are pleasures forevermore.[21] God's commands are not a burden, but a gift. "So the LORD commanded us to observe all these statutes, to fear the LORD our God *for our good always and for our survival.* . . ."[22] "This is love for God: to obey his commands. And his commands are not burdensome. . . ."[23]

This takes me back to the story earlier in the book about my son, Josiah. He wants to go where he is forbidden—the street in front of our home. Out of intense love and deep care, I command him not to play in the street. I don't suggest it; I command it. His life depends on following my commandment. Am I taking away his "fun" or "experience"? It may feel that way to him but in the big picture, my command and his obedience will save his life.

In the same vein, God commands us to not get near sexual sin. It's just too seductive. The street is too deadly. He's not commanding us with the attitude of "because I said so," as if He is holding out on us. He set apart a whole specific chapter of Proverbs (not to mention the majority of the previous two—Proverbs 5 and 6, also) to paint the canvas of ruin. And He approaches the subject again and again throughout the entire Bible. God is telling us for our own good. He longs for us to have true life. Thank God, He commands. He commands us not to ruin our lives.

THE APPLE OF MY EYE

Solomon adds, "Keep my teachings as *the apple* of your eye."[24] Think about it. When someone or something is the apple of your eye, your life revolves around him, her, or it. It is precious to you, indeed the most precious part of your life. It has captured your heart. My family (Christie and my two boys, Josiah and Titus) is the apple of my eye. God calls His children, Israel, the "apple of his eye."[25] The New Living translation states, "His most precious possession." The potency of "apple of his eye" is defined further in the next verse. God described Himself like a mother Eagle fluttering and hovering over her chicks "that spreads its wings to catch them and carries them on its pinions."[26]

When Solomon says the "apple of your eye," the literal translation is the "pupil" of your eye. That leaves no room for error or erring. There is nothing closer to the eye than the pupil. My pastor shared that Solomon is saying that our lives should revolve around God's Word. His Word before us and within us should be our most precious possession. There should be nothing more central to our lives than the Scriptures of God.

BEWARE OF HARDENING

If a man can read his Bible faithfully and commit serial murder, then beware. There is a graver danger than being ignorant of the Scriptures. That danger is being hardened to the Scriptures even as you read them daily. It's reading the Scriptures without a view of what God is saying about Himself and you. It's not taking time to "chew the cud," absorb, and apply what God is commanding of you. The apostle Paul writes,

> So get rid of all the filth and evil in your lives, and humbly accept the message God has planted in your hearts, for it is strong enough to save your souls.
>
> And remember it is a message to obey, not just to listen to. If you don't obey, you are only fooling yourselves. For if you listen and don't

obey, it is like looking at your face in a mirror but doing nothing to improve your appearance. You see yourself, walk away, and forget what you look like. But if you keep looking steadily into God's perfect law—the law that sets you free—and if you do what it says and don't forget what you heard, then God will bless you for doing it.[27]

In other words, God will bless you by keeping you from sexual ruin.

The more we become hardened to God's Word, the more God's Word hardens us. Albeit an extreme case, I believe BTK is proof. God's Word either melts the heart or hardens it. In terms of sexual sin, to become hardened to the truth of Scripture can bring catastrophic consequences. It can ruin your life.

INVENTORY

- ◆ What is the difference between reading God's Word and ruminating on God's Word? What does it look like for you personally to "chew the cud" of Scripture? When and how will you begin doing this?

- ◆ What does it mean to "treasure" God's Word in your life? How can you do this?

- ◆ Why might it be more dangerous to be numb to God's Word instead of ignorant of it?

- ◆ Right now, are you numb to God's Word? What can you do to change that?

HOPE IN RUIN
GRACE OVER GUILT

I wasn't planning on writing any more than chapter 13. I wasn't planning on this conclusion. But as I reflected over the book, I had the conviction that something was missing. This book was all about "how to avoid ruin" and not enough of a book on how to deal with it.

FALLEN

You've fallen to sexual sin. Or you've beat sexual sin for a time only to fail again. You've confessed. You've repented. But shame haunts you. Guilt smothers you. Despair conquers you. You feel that you've sinned so horribly and so often that your relationship with Jesus will never be whole again. You feel that He can never use you for His kingdom. You feel that you'll be free from guilt only if He punishes you in some way. Perhaps deep down, you feel that if you could just "pay your dues" then your guilt will go away.

These beliefs, thoughts, and feelings are lies. It's the Enemy accusing you. He is whispering, "You're disgusting. You're a pervert. God's done with you." Or, "You looked again? That's the third time this week! You're pitiful." Let me repeat, that's the Enemy accusing you.

Revelation 12:10b calls the Devil "the accuser of [the] brethren."[1] The accusations you hear and feel are not from your loving, forgiving, and gracious Father. They are from the Devil. The Devil hates you with a passion.

"Your adversary the Devil is prowling around like a roaring lion, looking for anyone he can devour."[2] The Devil wants you to buy into his lies that God is finished with you.

PUNISHED

You could never bear the punishment you deserve for any of your sin, including sexual sin: "Yet they cannot redeem themselves by paying a ransom to God. Redemption does not come so easily, for no one can pay enough . . . ."[3] No one can pay enough, that is, except Jesus. Jesus, the perfect Son of God, in the flesh took the full punishment of God's wrath for all the sins of your lifetime. The perfect, sinless, Jesus Christ became your sexual sin and died with it on the Cross: "For our sake [God] made Him to be sin who knew no sin, so that in Him we might become the righteousness of God."[4] "By sending His own Son in the likeness of sinful flesh and for sin, he condemned sin in the flesh . . . ."[5] Jesus embraced the rage and punishment of God on the Cross for all of your sexual sin—past, present, and future.

In the book of Colossians, the apostle Paul says, "You were dead because of your sins and because your sinful natures were not yet cut away. Then God made you alive with Christ, for he forgave all your sins."[6] You were spiritually dead. God made your spiritually dead heart beat through your faith. By your faith in the person and work of Jesus Christ, your sexual sin was conquered and devoured by Jesus' death and resurrection. By His mercy and love and through your faith in Jesus, you are saved and forgiven of your past, present, and future sins including sexual sins. So no matter what you did ten years ago, ten days ago, ten minutes ago, or ten minutes from now, that will never change the fact that "you have been justified by faith, [you] have peace with God through our Lord Jesus Christ."[7] "[T]here is *now* no condemnation for those who are in Christ Jesus."[8] Right now you are forgiven. Tomorrow you are forgiven. Your past, present, future sexual sins are covered in the blood of Jesus.

FREE TO SIN?

A word of warning here: Beware of playing the "I can sin because God has for-given me anyway" card. The author of Hebrews declares the evil of this belief by saying it's the same as "trampling on the Son of God."[9] Likewise, the apostle Paul confronted any thought of having "freedom" to sin in Romans 6:

> *Well, then, should we keep on sinning so that God can show us more and more of his wonderful grace? Of course not! Since we have died to sin, how can we continue to live in it?* Or have you forgotten that when we were joined with Christ Jesus in baptism, we joined him in his death? For we died and were buried with Christ by baptism. *And just as Christ was raised from the dead by the glorious power of the Father, now we also may live new lives.*
>
> Since we have been united with him in his death, we will also be raised to life as he was. *We know that our old sinful selves were cruci-fied with Christ so that sin might lose its power in our lives. We are no longer slaves to sin. For when we died with Christ we were set free from the power of sin.* And since we died with Christ, we know we will also live with him. We are sure of this because Christ was raised from the dead, and he will never die again. Death no longer has any power over him. *When he died, he died once to break the power of sin. But now that he lives, he lives for the glory of God. So you also should con-sider yourselves to be dead to the power of sin and alive to God through Christ Jesus.*[10]

If anyone declares they're "free" to continue a life in any kind of sexual immorality—*porneia*—then I would question their sincerity of repentance. If there has been no sincere repentance, there has been no salvation. Sorrow over sexual sin and repentance of sexual sin is the epic issue.

Paul contrasts godly sorrow and worldly sorrow. Godly sorrow brings repentance, salvation, heart transformation, and *life change*. Worldly sorrow brings sadness and embarrassment over having gotten caught in sexual sin.

"For the kind of sorrow God wants us to experience leads us away from sin and results in salvation. There's no regret for that kind of sorrow. But worldly sorrow, which lacks repentance, results in spiritual death."[11] True sorrow, godly sorrow, leads to repentance. True repentance leads to a transformed heart. A transformed heart leads to the desire for godliness. This is all a work of God's grace. And for anyone to use "God's grace" as a license to continue in sexual sin, the author of Hebrews calls it an insult to God and His grace of epic proportions.[12]

THE BATTLE

Are you sorrowful over your sexual sin? Are you repentant? Most of you who have read this are sorrowful, repentant, and you long to be holy in your thoughts and life. But still you battle. You find yourself lonely at 11:30 p.m. on a Friday night and succumb to the temptation of Internet porn. As Paul says about himself in Romans 7, you find yourself doing what you don't want to do. But here's the kicker: you *don't* want to do it, right? You are overwhelmed with sorrow and guilt every time. You know it breaks the heart of God. So you fight. Yes, you get knocked to the canvas. Sometimes you get a 2-count, sometimes an 8-count. But still you fight. I plead with you to keep fighting. So would Pastor John Piper. Pastor Piper expressed it perfectly,

> [F]aith will fight anything that gets between it and Christ. The distinguishing mark of saving faith is not perfection. The mark of faith is not that I never sin sexually. The mark of faith is that I fight. I fight anything that dims my sight of Jesus as my glorious Savior. I fight anything that diminishes the fullness of the lordship of Jesus in my life. I fight anything that threatens to replace Jesus as the supreme Treasure of my life. Anything that stands between me and receiving Jesus faith fights—not with fists or knives or guns or bombs, but with the truth of Christ.[13]

FREEDOM FROM GUILT

Don't curl up on the floor of guilt. Jesus didn't die just to free you from sin, but also from guilt. Jesus took your sin and guilt on the cross. You are justi-fied—declared "not guilty"—before God because of your faith in the person and work of Jesus.

Don't believe the lies of the Enemy when he tells you that you're disgusting and condemned and you'll always be a slave to porn. He's a liar. He's hell-bent on making you doubt that you're free and forgiven in Christ. He wants to kill you with guilt. So he accuses you ruthlessly. But accusations are all the power he has. He has no reign over you. Again, the apostle Paul in Colossians,

> [God] canceled the record that contained the charges against us. He took it and destroyed it by nailing it to Christ's cross. In this way God disarmed the evil rulers and authorities. He shamed them pub-licly by his victory over them on the cross of Christ.[14]

Satan is an imposter. He's acting as witness (accuser), judge, and jury over your life. He takes the list of charges of sexual sin against you, shakes it in your face, and screams "guilty!" Yet the only One who has the right and authority to judge you and condemn you is Christ Jesus. And here is what God's Word has to say about that:

> Who then will condemn us? Will Christ Jesus? No, for he is the one who died for us and was raised to life for us and is sitting at the place of highest honor next to God, pleading for us.[15]

Instead of shaking the warrant of sexual sin in your face, Jesus put it in His hand and had it nailed with Him on the cross. Again, Pastor Piper:

> Make sure you see this most glorious of all truths: God took the record of all your sins—all your sexual failures—that made you a

debtor to wrath, and instead of holding them up in front of your face and using them as the warrant to send you to hell, he put them in the palm of his Son's hand and nailed them to the cross.[16]

LIES, LIES

Still the enemy is relentless. He'll distract and burden you often by reminding you of that warrant—bringing to your mind your sexual sin and the guilt. Concerning the Enemy, take heart in the words of Paul,

> [God] took [the record that contained charges against us] and destroyed it by nailing it to Christ's cross. *In this way God disarmed the evil rulers and authorities. He shamed them publicly by his victory over them on the cross of Christ.*[17]

Christ disarmed the Devil and his demons. And he shamed them. In Colossians 2:15, Paul is using a word picture to drive home his point. When the Roman military conquered a foreign country in war, there would be a parade of celebration in honor of the military hero. The judges of Rome would lead the parade. Following the judges would be those trumpeting the victory. Next came the spoils of the war—silver, gold, animals, prisoners, and so forth. Following the spoils came the conquered enemy king. The prisoners and enemy king were paraded through the streets stripped in humiliation. Next came the victorious army's officials along with musicians and dancers. Then finally came the military hero himself, in all his battle array and glory. He was the champion. And all the people celebrated him.

See the picture? The enemy king and his prisoners publicly humiliated and the hero celebrated? That is the picture Paul is painting of what Jesus did through the Cross. Jesus is the champion. He lived the sinless life, joyfully and voluntarily died a brutal death on the cross for your sin, and rose as the hero conquering sin, death, and the Devil. In so doing, the spiritual reality is that He stripped the Devil and his demons bare of power and made fools out of them. The Phillips translation renders it this way,

". . .[Jesus] exposed them, shattered, empty, and defeated, in his final glorious triumphant act!"

So when the Enemy brings guilt into your gut through his accusations, get your Bible and turn to Colossians 2:13-15. Pray it, plead it, preach it to yourself. Jesus took on your sin and guilt through his death on the cross, rose from the grave, and in so doing the Devil and his liars were paraded around naked and defeated. This Enemy is a shamed loser and has no power over you. Picture yourself standing with your foot on the neck of the Enemy. Believe it, declare it to yourself, and be free!

Don't grovel in guilt over your sexual failure. Don't be defeated. Don't give up. Jesus beat sin and guilt. He was raised from the dead to prove it. He's the hero. You are united with Jesus in the victory. Let your thoughts of punishment in order to your ease guilt die with Jesus on the cross. Jesus bore the punishment that you deserved for your sexual sin once and for all. The Enemy has been defeated and shamed. You are free and a champion because you are united with The Champion. To hold these truths to heart will keep you off the canvas of guilt. As Pastor Piper expresses it, "[W]hen you learn to deal with the guilt of sexual failure this way, you will fall less often. Because Christ will become increasingly precious to you."[18]

Cherish Christ. Treasure who you are in Christ. Rest in His grace. Be free from your guilt. His grace conquered guilt.

APPENDIX

CHAPTER 6

Below is an online article written by Randy Alcorn titled: "Deterring Immorality by Counting Its Cost: An Exorbitant Price of Sexual Sin." Within the article he shares a personalized list of what sexual sin would cost him. He even personalizes the list with the names of his wife and daughters to express sexual sin's direct impact on his life and family. Alcorn is also a minister so you will see application related to that field also. I'd suggest you simply insert the names of those who would apply to you, and the field to which it would apply also. I encourage you, as Pastor Alcorn does, to take this list and make it your own.

PERSONALIZED LIST OF ANTICIPATED CONSEQUENCES OF IMMORALITY

- Grieving my Lord; displeasing the One whose opinion most matters.

- Dragging into the mud Christ's sacred reputation.

- Loss of reward and commendation from God.

- Having to one day look Jesus in the face at the judgment seat and give an account of why I did it.

- Forcing God to discipline me in various ways.

- Following in the footsteps of men I know of whose immorality forfeited their ministry and caused me to shudder. List of these names:

- Suffering of innocent people around me who would get hit by my shrapnel (a la Achan [Joshua 7]).

- Untold hurt to Nanci, my best friend and loyal wife.

- Loss of Nanci's respect and trust.

- Hurt to and loss of credibility with my beloved daughters, Karina and Angela. ("Why listen to a man who betrayed Mom and us?")

- If my blindness should continue or my family be unable to forgive, I could lose my wife and my children forever.

- Shame to my family. ("Why isn't Daddy a pastor anymore?"; the cruel comments of others who would invariably find out.)

- Shame to my church family.

- Shame and hurt to my fellow pastors and elders. List of names:

- Shame and hurt to my friends, and especially those I've led to Christ and discipled. List of names:

- Guilt awfully hard to shake. Even though God would forgive me, would I forgive myself?

- Plaguing memories and flashbacks that could taint future intimacy with my wife.

- Disqualifying myself after having preached to others.

- Surrender of the things I am called to and love to do—teach and preach and write and minister to others. Forfeiting forever certain opportunities to serve God. Years of training and experience in ministry wasted for a long period of time, maybe permanently.

- Being haunted by my sin as I look in the eyes of others, and having it all dredged up again wherever I go and whatever I do.

- Undermining the hard work and prayers of others by saying to our community "this is a hypocrite—who can take seriously anything he and his church have said and done?"

- Laughter, rejoicing, and blasphemous smugness by those who disrespect God and the church (2 Samuel 12:14).

- Bringing great pleasure to Satan, the Enemy of God.

- Heaping judgment and endless problems on the person I would have committed adultery with.

- Possible diseases: gonorrhea, syphilis, chlamydia, herpes, and AIDS (pain, constant reminder to me and my wife, possible infection of Nanci, or in the case of AIDS, even causing her death, as well as mine.)

- Possible pregnancy, with its personal and financial implications, including a lifelong reminder of sin to me and my family.

- Loss of self-respect, discrediting my own name, and invoking shame and lifelong embarrassment upon myself.

These are only some of the consequences. If only we would rehearse in advance the ugly and overwhelming consequences of immorality, we would be far more prone to avoid it. May we live each day in the love and fear of God.[1]

After reading this, how does this make you feel?

Which things were pointed out that impacted you the most? The least?

Notes

CHAPTER 1

1. Psalm 101:2b-4 NASB.
2. Proverbs 7:7.

CHAPTER 2

1. NKJV.
2. Ephesians 5:3a NIV.
3. Colossians 3:5.
4. Song of Songs 7:6, 7b, 10-12.
5. I would add that sexual exploration between spouses should be done in faith. In other words, they should have peace that God has granted them freedom to enjoy each other's bodies in the context of "oneness." However, if the conscience of the husband or wife is bothered or convicted then the sexual exploration is not being done in faith. And according to Paul in Romans 14:23c, "[E]verything that is not done in faith is sin."
6. Genesis 2:23-25. I would suggest simply asking one another if their ideas of sexual play would bring more depth, joy, fun, excitement, to their "oneness."
7. Galatians 5:24 NIV.
8. Galatians 5:23
9. Romans 6:12-13a.
10. Romans 12:1.

CHAPTER 3

1. Kevin Sanders, "Timothy Treadwell and Girlfriend Killed by Grizzly in Alaska," 10/14/2003 http://www.yellowstone-bearman.com/bearupd.html#timtreadwell; accessed June 12, 2005.
2. Ibid.
3. 1 Peter 5:8b.
4. 1 Peter 5:8a.
5. 2 Corinthians 2:11.
6. Proverbs 7:10, 13-21.
7. Proverbs 7:12.
8. 1 Corinthians 10:13b.
9. NASB.
10. Proverbs 7:25.

CHAPTER 4

1. Proverbs 7:19.
2. James 1:14-16.
3. Job 24:15.

4. Proverbs 5:21.

5. Galatians 6:7.

6. Mark 4:22.

7. 1 Corinthians 6:13c.

8. Hebrews 12:7-11 HCSB.

CHAPTER 5

1. Sentence adapted from the following quote by Dr. Robert Weiss, director of the Sexual Recovery Institute, Los Angeles, California, "Cyber-sex is the crack cocaine of sexual addiction." Quote found in article by Raymond Chan, Emily Reyna, Matt Rubens, and Annie Wu in *Online Pornography: More Than Just Dirty Pictures*, Stanford University Class Project, Internet http://cse.stanford.edu/class/cs201/projects-00-01/pornography/addiction.htm; accessed October 23, 2007.

2. Raymond Chan, Emily Reyna, Matt Rubens, and Annie Wu in *Online Pornography: More Than Just Dirty Pictures*, Stanford University Class Project, Internet http://cse.stanford.edu/class/cs201/projects-00-01/pornography/addiction.htm; accessed October 23, 2007.

3. Illusions: Uncovering the Truth about Pornography. http://www.illusionsprogram.net/youve-been-exposed.html; accessed April 17, 2008. The Web page cites its source of information as taken from "Brain Pathways," Douglas Weiss, PhD.

4. Hebrews 4:12 HCSB.

5. Jeremiah 23:29.

6. Proverbs 7:1.

7. Colossians 4:2 my emphasis.

8. Proverbs 27:17.

9. Proverbs 27:6.

10. Proverbs 4:24 my emphasis.

11. The name of the program is X3watch. "X3watch is accountability software designed to help with online integrity. When you browse the Internet and access a site which may contain questionable material, the program will record the site name. A person of your choice (an accountability partner) will receive an e-mail containing all questionable sites you may have visited." Visit www.x3watch.com for more information.

12. Hebrews 12:2.

13. Galatians 2:20; Romans 8:9-11.

14. Romans 6:4-14.

CHAPTER 6

1. Proverbs 7:22.

2. Proverbs 4:23.

3. Proverbs 27:17, 6.

4. Matthew 5:19.

5. Psalm 51:10.

6. Philippians 4:8.

7. Job 31:1.

CHAPTER 7

1. Phillip Buam, "Vesna Vulovic: How to Survive a Bombing at 33,000 Feet," http://www.avsec. com/interviews/vesna-vulovic.htm; accessed May 7, 2008.
2. Proverbs 7:26.
3. Galatians 6:7-8a.
4. Proverbs 7:27.
5. 1 Corinthians 9:27.
6. Proverbs 7:27 HCSB.
7. Ephesians 2:8-9.
8. Romans 6:1-2.
9. Matthew 7:21; 1 John 2:19.
10. 2 Corinthians 7:10.
11. Romans 1:18.
12. Romans 1:24.
13. Romans 1:26.
14. Romans 1:28-32.

CHAPTER 8

1. Proverbs 2:18.
2. Proverbs 5:3-5a.
3. Proverbs 6: 26-29.
4. Proverbs 7:1-2.
5. Proverbs 7:6-7.

CHAPTER 9

1. Joel Rosenthal. Interview with Andrew Bacevich, April 9, 2003. http://www.cceia.org/resources/transcripts/925.html; accessed August 16, 2007.
2. "The Obstinate Lighthouse" http://www.snopes.com/military/lighthouse.asp; accessed April 18, 2008.
3. Shaunti Feldhahn, *For Women Only: What You Need to Know about the Inner Lives of Men* (Sisters, Oregon: Multnomah, 2004), 133.
4. Genesis 25:29-33.
5. Hebrews 2:16-17.
6. Proverbs 27:7.
7. Ephesians 4:6-7.
8. Romans 11:35.
9. Philippians 4:11-13.
10. John 10:10.
11. Ecclesiastes 4:10-12.
12. Psalm 25:26.
13. Proverbs 17:17a NASB.
14. Mark Buchanan, *The Rest of God: Restoring your Soul by Restoring Sabbath* (Nashville: W Publishing Group, 2006), 93.

15. Proverbs 7:25.
16. Proverbs 7:9.
17. Proverbs 7:21.

CHAPTER 10

1. Proverbs 7:10
2. Ibid.
3. Proverbs 7:16.

CHAPTER 11

1. Hebrews 13:4 NIV.
2. Claudia Willis, Kristina Dell, with reporting by Alice Park/New York, "What Makes Teens Tick; A flood of hormones, sure. But also a host of structural changes in the brain. Can those explain the behaviors that make adolescence so exciting—and so exasperating?" http://www. deathpenaltyinfo.org/article.php?scid=27&did=977; accessed April 17, 2008. The online article was taken from May 10, 2004, *Time* magazine.
3. Ephesians 5:3a NIV.
4. Song of Songs 2:7c; 3:5c; 8:4b NIV.
5. Proverbs 7:13-14.
6. 1 Corinthians 16:13 NASB, my emphasis.

CHAPTER 12

1. Genesis 2:16-17 NASB.
2. Genesis 3:1c NASB.
3. Genesis 3:12 NASB.
4. Genesis 3:13b NASB.
5. Genesis 2:17; 3:17-24.
6. Proverbs 7:13a.
7. James 1:14-16 NASB.
8. James 1:14-16.
9. Proverbs 7:13.
10. Proverbs 7:15.
11. 1 Corinthians 6:13 NASB.

CHAPTER 13

1. 1 Kings 11:4.
2. Ecclesiastes 1:2.
3. Ecclesiastes 2:1.
4. Ecclesiastes 2:8.
5. Ecclesiastes 2:11b.
6. Proverbs 7:1-2 NASB.
7. Proverbs 7:1b NASB.

8. John 15: 1-17.
9. Psalm 1:2.
10. Donna M. Amaral-Phillips , "Why Do Cattle Chew Their Cud?", http://www.uky.edu/Ag/
    AnimalSciences/dairy/extension/nut00014.pdf; accessed April 23, 2008.
11. Communication and Educational Technology Services, University of Minnesota Extension,
    "Ruminant Anatomy and Physiology," http://www.extension.umn.edu/distribution/
    livestocksystems/components/DI0469- 02.html; accessed April 23, 2008.
12. Psalm 1:1a NASB.
13. Psalm 1:2 ESV my emphasis.
14. My emphasis.
15. My emphasis.
16. Hebrews 4:12.
17. Psalm 119:18.
18. Psalm 19:7-9.
19. Donna M. Amaral-Phillips, "Why Do Cattle Chew Their Cud?"
20. Proverbs 7:1b-2a NASB.
21. Psalm 16:11.
22. Deuteronomy 6:24 NASB my emphasis.
23. 1 John 5:3 NIV.
24. Proverbs 7:2.
25. Deuteronomy 32:10 NIV.
26. Deuteronomy 32:11 NIV.
27. James 1:21-25.

CONCLUSION

1. NASB.
2. 1 Peter 5:8b HCSB.
3. Psalm 49:7-8.
4. 2 Corinthians 5:21 ESV my emphasis.
5. Romans 8:3b NASB.
6. Colossians 2:13.
7. Romans 5:1 NASB.
8. Romans 8:1 NASB my emphasis.
9. Hebrews 10:29.
10. Romans 6:1-10 my emphasis.
11. 2 Corinthians 7:10.
12. Hebrews 10:26-31.
13. John Piper, excerpt taken from message, "How to Deal with Gutsy Guilt of Sexual Failure for the
    Glory of Christ and His Global Cause," preached by Pastor Piper of Bethlehem Baptist Church,
    Minneapolis, Minnesota, at the Passion '07 College Conference main session, January 4, 2007, in
    Atlanta, Georgia. A transcript of his full message can be found at the following Web site: http://www.
    desiringgod.org/ResourceLibrary/ConferenceMessages/ByDate/1927_Howto_Deal_with_the_Guilt_
    of_Sexual_Failure_for_the_Glory_of_Christ_and_His_Global_Cause/; accessed April 25, 2008.

14. Colossians 2:14-15.

15. Romans 8:34.

16. Piper, message excerpt from "How to Deal with Gutsy Guilt of Sexual Failure for the Glory of Christ and His Global Cause."

17. Colossians 2:15 my emphasis.

18. Piper, message excerpt from "How to Deal with Gutsy Guilt of Sexual Failure for the Glory of Christ and His Global Cause."

APPENDIX

1. Randy Alcorn, "Deterring Immorality by Counting Its Cost: An Exorbitant Price of Sexual Sin," 2006, Eternal Perspective Ministries. http://www.epm.org/articles/leadpur2.html; accessed March 4, 2008.

Acknowledgments

To my godly and gorgeous wife, Christie: Thank you, baby-love, for your incredible patience and understanding as I have labored on this project. I'm back from the dead now. Thanks for keeping dinner warm for me. I love you.

To Mom, Dad, and my sister, Tyree: Your selflessness and support is unrelenting. Words just won't do. I love you. Thank you.

To John A. (Lex) Williamson, Jr.: I can't express enough how much I appreciate your incredibly generous donation to make possible the printing and publishing of this book. I hope my heartfelt "thank you" says enough. Rest assured that God is going to use this book powerfully in the lives of people, especially men, young and old, single and married. God will see to it that your gift is not in vain.

To my ministry staff: Brandon Gilbert, Gresham Hill, Jacob Henley, Scott Crews, and Wes Wages. Thank you, my brothers, for taking much time and energy to read over this material again and again. Thanks for your incredible insights and counsel. I loved the frustration and laughter we shared sitting in a circle all day long going page by page through the book. "McDonalds" —hilarious. Monell's baby!

To Jacob: Thank you for the long hours and the incredible hard work you invested into the creativity and administration of this project. It spoke volumes of your belief in this message and your desire to get it into people's lives. You encouraged me well along the way but your excellence and investment into the work said it all. It's an honor to serve with you brother.

To Gresham: Thank you for pushing me to complete this work. I greatly appreciate your availability, counsel, encouragement, and sacrifice throughout this project. I'm thankful for our years of partnership—good times and tough times. You are a dear friend.

To my fellow pastors, youth pastors, and friends, who read clips of the book and gave great counsel and suggestions: a man-hug to all of you.

To my church family—Shades Mountain Independent Church, our small group, and SMI's Compass college and young adults' leaders and ministry under whom I serve: Christie and I treasure you. Go Compass! Eh-hem…

To Bob Moon: You will always show up somewhere in my ramblings if I have anything to do with it. Your love, support, and influence on me since a teenager will never be forgotten. God used you a long time ago to detour me from ruining my life.

To my brothers in Christ, young and old, single and married, from east coast to west coast, and all over the world, for sharing with me your struggles and championing this book: I'm praying for you not to ruin your life. Pray for me.

To my sons—Josiah and Titus: For coming into my office as I study and write, crawling into my lap, and snuggling with me at the best possible times —and the worst possible times. You both are the delight of my heart.

To Jesus: The only One who beat sin, death, and ruin. Thank You for Your grace to conquer ruin, and survive it. To You be the glory!

Jarrod Jones lives in Alabama with his wife Christie, and two boys, Josiah and Titus. In 2003 Jarrod graduated from Southern Baptist Theological Seminary at Louisville, Kentucky, with his masters of divinity degree. Every year, Jarrod speaks before thousands all across the world at churches, conferences, retreats, camps, and school assemblies. Jarrod is also the author of *The Backward Life: In Pursuit of an Uncommon Faith* (Revell).

For more information on Jarrod or to order other Jarrod Jones books and merchandise visit WWW.JARRODJONES.COM.

To order books in bulk at discounted rates, contact INFO@GRESHAMHILL.COM.

To schedule Jarrod to speak for your next event, contact: INFO@GRESHAMHILL.COM.

For more information on Jarrod's books visit: WWW.13WAYSTORUINYOURLIFE.COM

WWW.BACKWARDLIFE.COM